Fact
and
Fiction

Fiction and Reality

R. Evans Pansing

ISBN: 978-1-4669-3704-8 (sc)
ISBN: 978-1-4669-3703-1 (e)

Trafford rev. 05/14/2012

 www.trafford.com

North America & international
toll-free: 1 888 232 4444 (USA & Canada)
phone: 250 383 6864 ♦ fax: 812 355 4082

CONTENTS

THE GRANDFATHER CLOCK

E VERY CHILD HAS A TIME in their life when they
are certain that a person or personage inhabits
their bedroom in the nighttime season. This child has a
very active imagination. He is a boy living at home with his
family, mother, dad, and his younger siblings. The events
began when the boy was about five or six years old.

The days were filled with a lot of excitement and activity.
Family gatherings always made for lots of visions that were
cast about by relatives. Scary stories about near misses as
well as trips or unusual people met while traveling. Relatives
long gone that had ridden through history with adventure
and hard times. Grandfather Abernathy was held up as an
example of many adventures and activities. All of this was
heard and assimilated by young ears attached to the head of
our impressionable boy on this particular day. As the day
wore on the boy wore out. His folks sent him to bed when
he started to nod his head in exhaustion.

Our boy needed no rocking chair to send him off to the
land of Nod. Deep sleep comes first and when the body and
mind recover, then the sleeper begins to rise to the surface
of foggy consciousness. Our boy was awakened at 2 AM
by his assurance that some one was in his room. He kept
hearing a bumping sound in the night. Bump! Bump! Maybe
someone was hitting his or her head under his bed. He knew
by instinct it was not any of his family. Not moving a muscle
and effecting shallow breathing our boy waited for further
developments. He waited for what seemed like an eternity
of time. When he was certain the monster had left, he ran to
his parents room for consolation and protection.

"Dad! Dad! A monster was in my room!"

A loving but annoyed father came up out of the bed covers with the exclamation, for this event was a repeat of many others just like it.

"Son, it was just a dream. You just had a bad dream."

"No dad, I could hear him moving about under my bed. It went bump, bump. Can I sleep with you and Mom?"

"No son. I'll come over and check out your room."

Therefore, the father went to his son's room for the inspection that would satisfy a young boy's vivid imagination.

"See! He is not under the bed." The father said, as he swept a broom handle all about the area under the bed.

"Maybe he went into the closet to hide." The boy offered up as a reasonable conclusion. Where upon dad made a very detailed and graphic search of the closet to demonstrate no one could hide from his exhaustive examination. When the little fellow was reassured that no monster or stranger was in his room he returned to his bed with kisses and assurances from his father that "all was well," in his room.

"Thanks dad," he said, "but leave the light on in case you want to come back to check on me later."

The boy might be young, but he was also wise beyond his years.

The father left, and the boy began to relax, readying for sleep. He tried to keep one eye open, just in case. This did not work for long as the sandman made his visit with armloads of sleep sand.

The days and weeks that followed were very normal, and uneventful in the

Monster department. The young boy did examine his room each night before going to sleep, but he convinced his folks to install a night light in his room so he wouldn't stub his toes when using the bathroom at night. It was a good plan that was working.

Just as summer was at its height, the boy's bedroom window was opened wide to allow the cooler breezes from out side, to cool down his hot upstairs bedchamber. Our boy was slightly leery of the open window arrangement but made no comment to his parents because he had his night-light. He also had appropriated a ping-pong paddle for extra protection. Well hidden under the sheet where his hands gripped the paddle until his little fingers went numb. Finally, sleep over took him, and he relaxed the paddle. Just after midnight, that's when the old grandfather clock struck twelve, our boy was awakened as he heard the stirrings of something coming in the window. Holding his breath, he waited to be murdered in his own bed. After a long time the boy became certain that, the intruder had hidden in the closet.

More stirrings and then a long lull. When he felt like the intruder had left the way, it was a time the boy acted. Throwing off the sheet with a whoop, the boy ran down the hall and into his parent's bedroom with the terrible news.

"Mom! Dad! The monster has returned!"

Patiently the mother got up at the urging of dad. He was heard to say, "it's your turn."

Mother took son by the hand and returned to the room of the little melodrama. With a flair that would have been fit for a knight in shinning armor, she dissected every foot of the closet. No person was found, only a disarray of toys and clothes, hastily placed there by a boy in a hurry. Under the bed also proved to be void of any being.

Mother began her duty of instruction.

"Son, there is nothing or no one in your closet. Only a messy place that would frighten anyone trying to hide there. All of this business about monsters in your room is just a lot of BUNK. You can't keep this up. You are disturbing your father's much needed sleep. We have come many times at your request and have found nothing amiss. You are getting too old for this. Please no more false alarms."

Mother was as stern as she could be and yet felt saddened her son was having such a difficult time growing up. The young boy had a tear coming that tumbled down a trembling cheek.

With trembling voice, the young boy struck a familiar note of all of us. "May I sleep with you and dad tonight?"

Mothers are known for soft hearts from children's pleas.

"Be very still and do not wake your dad. This will be the last time this scenario will work. After this, you will have to deal with your dreams and imaginations yourself. You are a big boy now and must shoulder the truth that no one would pick out our little house to burgle or to scare young boys. You are too old for this foolishness."

For a long time the boy had no scary dreams or apparitions in the night. No occasions to call his parents about monsters or burglars coming in his room. Only once did he call out in the night for assistance when he had heard a stirring in the old grandfather clock. His dad got up and took him to the clock to assure him of no monsters. No need to open the glass door for you could see right through to the pendulum.

"Son, this old clock was built by my grandfather Abernasty. Your great grandfather. He was a carpenter and built tables and chairs and furniture of all kinds. When he didn't have furniture to sell, he would make caskets from the spare wood in his shop. He also built clock cases like the one before us out of all kinds of spare lumber in the shop, and you can't sleep in my bed tonight."

This was quite a revelation to the boy. Casket wood in the clock made it available to all kinds of spooky things, he thought.

Dad and boy each returned to their own rooms to finish their nights rest. All was quiet.

Months passed, and the boy thought the intruder had moved out. He was awakened one night as the old clock chimed in an unusual way. The clock sounded as though it was muffled when the midnight striking took place. The boy wondered if his parents had noticed the flat chimes. Nothing moved or made a sound for a considerable length of time. Now that he was older, the boy had acquired a certain amount of bravery when the sounds of the night reached his ears. He got up and quietly skulked down the hall to the old grandfather clock.

Opening the glass front door, he was met by a person of an unusual appearance. He was very small and very thin. His face was not so ugly as it was comical. He might have been a clown. Bulbous nose and beady eyes and a round mouth that spoke.

"Well, we finally meet. My name is BUNK and I have had to move around a lot because of your parents' searches. He almost got me with that broom handle under the bed long ago, but I hung on the bed slats for dear life."

The boy saw a movement behind Bunk. Bunk pulled the person behind him out and introduced him as his brother, Bump. Little Bump was even more comical with buggy eyes and whiskers. His nose was flat and almost pig-like. His hair was spiky and looked like wood shavings only orange.

The boy's nerves were being tested but held steady after this new introduction. Inside he was wanting to laugh or giggle but held his peace. He had to pinch himself to be sure, what was happening was not a dream. He felt nothing as he made the effort for pinching. He hoped his chattering teeth and wobbly knees were not noticed. Just when the boy was going to excuse himself for some parental intervention, movement behind the clock's two weird residents made the boy tense up.

"Oh," said Bunk." This is our dog Rags."

A strange looking mutt poked his head out from between the two clowns to impart to the boy a muffled growl of the non-threatening variety. Gray hair that spiked up all over his body so that he looked like an old hairbrush, with bristles missing. A square jaw that was rather large for a little dog. Hanging from his jaw were threads of fabric making his mouth a hodgepodge of color. All in all the entire dog was ugly.

"Rags goes with us on our many forays about the houses were we are billeted. We are ready to go out tonight to affect our mischief. Would you like to go with us?"

The boy sucked in some air and slowly exhaled while asking." What do you do when carousing around the house?"

Bump replied, "Come with us and see."

With that comment, the group of four slowly moved down the hall into the parents' bedroom. The boy whispered to the others," you can't go in there."

Bunk replied that Rags needed his daily rations. With that, they all moved into the room with stealth. Bunk and Bump opened father's sock drawer where the dog Rags began to nose around until he found a pair of blue socks. He would eat one and leave the other one intact. He then found a pair of argyle socks that were treated in the same way. Rags ate one and left the other one intact. This procedure continued for a while when the boy noticed Bunk taking his fathers glasses and hiding them behind the dresser. Finally, they left the room and headed downstairs.

"What was that all about," the boy asked?

"Oh, we just help things along to make life challenging for folks."

Downstairs the two clown-like fellows tapped on light bulbs to make them extinguish when turned on. Rags found some batteries that his fiercely intense hot breath rendered them useless for the next person that needed one for an electronic application. Plumbing was modified so that faucets leaked. This went on until the boy said he thought that was enough for one night. The others agreed since it had been a long time between their nighttime mischievous forays.

"Usually we effect a lot more havoc but for your sake we will stop for this night. Drawers that won't close, plugged up drains, potted plants withering mysteriously, gum in the carpet and much more is our usual activity, as well as scaring young boys with ripe imaginations," said Bump as he led Rags by the scruff of the neck.

They all returned to the upstairs hall and said their goodnights at the old coffin clock's front panel as the clock struck a fine sounding, **ONE!**

Our young boy returned to his bed with a thousand thoughts going through his mind at breakneck speed. In the morning, he was uncertain of the events of the previous night. His wondering was cut short as he heard his dad asking about where his glasses were and has anybody seen his other argyle sock.

Eventually the boy made a few journeys with his newfound friends from the clock, but the intervals became so great and lengthier, that he could only imagine what had happened to him those long ago nights.

One night, after a very long interval, he got up and went to the clock to see whether anyone was at home. The case was empty except for the three weights hanging on their chains and the pendulum. He noticed a small scrap of paper and when looking at it saw it to be only gibberish. He returned to his room and by accident held it up by his dresser mirror. The note came into focus as it had been written as a mirror image.

"We have left to go to another house with a much younger boy in residence. Don't forget us and do expect to hear from us again when you marry and have a young boy yourself. your friends BUNK, BUMP and RAGS"

TOMMY'S BRIDGE

THE SCHOOL BUS WAS JUST cresting the little hill that led down to Tommy's farm. He held his breath because of the possibility that Old Stony Creek was out of its banks and flooding the ford that led to his home. This morning the water was rising. Maybe his dad was waiting for him on the big farm tractor. The tractor could ford the stream when the stream was about three feet. The old Dodge couldn't get through because it was too low. If the stream was too high, Tommy would have to trudge back up the hill to the McPeak farm and stay the night there. It was all prearranged as he had gone through this scenario frequently in the past, when he was younger. Standing up in the bus he strained to see the results of the spring rains, and snow melts from the mountains. His heart sank as the stream was very high and no Dad on the tractor was in sight.

Tommy exited the bus and looked over the stream for any sign of his parents. The air was cold, and the wind was constant so it took only Tommy a second to determine that he would have to walk back up the road and intrude on the McPeak's for a night's lodging.

The McPeaks were a nice enough family but Tommy hated to intrude upon the family for such a trivial reason. Cog McPeak was the dad. He was called Cog because years ago in a grain mill he caught his shirt in a cog that tore off all his clothes to the amusement of his fellow workers. He was called Cog ever after. They had one daughter a few years older than Tommy. Her name was Gertrude, but everyone called her Girlie.

Girlie was thin and gangly with an aquiline nose and wide eyes, complete with ugly round yellow glasses to better spy on others. She had a high flat forehead and a grin that was more lemon than sugar. Girlie was what you would call plain and goosey. Each night after supper she would retire to her room and sulk or read or something. She avoided her family as well as guests. Tommy was glad.

The McPeak boy was two years younger than Tommy. His name was Peter, but everyone called him Wee. He was small for his age and chubby. He had a high round forehead and close set piggy eyes. He was small of stature and had a slight stutter as well as quivering lips. He wore glasses so thick that one easily surmised his eyes were weak. Wee being so small was always looking for attention. This made him a first-class pest. When Tommy was in attendance, Wee pestered Tommy for all kinds of information or requested participation in games etc. ("Look at my Barlow knife and tell me what you think, etc.")

Mr. McPeak would read his paper and smoke his pipe each evening without a word. He would change his routine only when he turned on the big, stand in the corner Philco radio to listen to Fibber McGee and Molly or Jack Benny. Amos and Andy were also a favorite for Cog. Sometimes he would laugh so hard and he bellowed so loud it caused Mrs. McPeak to scold him.

Tommy knocked on the door and Mrs. McPeak answered immediately as though she were expecting him.

"Come on in Tommy we've been expecting you. Wee was certain you would be back up the hill, and he is waiting for you in the dinning room."

Oh no, thought Tommy as he hung up his coat and cap. Wee would have some model boat or plane scattered all over the table and expected Tommy to read the instructions. Wee would expect Tommy to glue the small intricate parts to Wee's exact specifications. It would be another long night opined Tommy.

Supper was good as usual because Mrs. McPeak was a good cook. She liked to be called Bea because her real name was Beatrice. She wanted to be called Mom when Tommy first started staying overnight but the thought stuck in Tommy's throat. Now that Tommy was older he called her Bea. She was very good at locating one's short comings and then giving corrective advice. Tommy was corrected often and thoroughly.

After supper the family split up. Girlie went to her room and Wee coerced Tommy to help with homework. Mr. McPeak eventually turned on the radio, thereby giving Tommy some respite from homework duties.

After the radio shows, Tommy excused himself and retired to Wee's room. The McPeaks set up a cot for Wee in the parents bedroom. Tommy was always directed to sleep in Wee's room. One of Tommy's complaints, to himself, was that the boy's room always smelled of lavender and apple's blossoms. This night it was very cold and the bed was small but warm. Tommy was growing taller and when he stretched out fully his feet touched something woody at the foot of the bed. Diving headfirst he dodged under the covers to retrieve the woody piece. He grabbed the lavender branch and as he retrieved it, his nose was pressed against the bottom sheet covering the mattress. Suddenly, he realized why Wee was called Wee. The branch was a piece of lavender with dried blossoms. This along with the apple scented candles gave the room and bed a sense of respectability. Wee had a weak bladder as well as weak eyes. Tommy slept that night on top of the covers with only the comforter to keep warm. The night was long but filled with a determination that would change his life.

Tommy left the next morning for school with a new resolve. He was going to build a walking cable bridge over Stony Creek, or his name was not Thomas Seagood Evans. As the bus passed the ford, he saw his dad on the farm tractor indicating by signs that the would be waiting for him after school this day.

At school Tommy was always looking for a girl he had a crush on. Casey Castle was her name. Everyone called her Casey Since her full name was Katherine Cavanaugh Castle. (K.C.C.) Her family founded the town of Castle decades ago.

Old Mr. Castle came to the crossroads years ago and saw that it would be a good place to start a feed and lumber yard. When the yard was built, he hired workers that stayed and built houses. This caused a general store to spring up with more citizens and houses. The town continued to prosper with a saloon, barbershop, a livery, black smith etc. Now it has a post office and schoolhouse. The school was small with grades one through twelve. About a hundred students attended all the grades.

He finally saw Casey with other classmates clustered about her. He walked past the group with all kinds of visions in his head. Trying for Casey's attention would have to wait. His vision now would be to build a bridge, and nothing was going to side track his resolve. No frivolity for him now. He would have to spend time at the library for information concerning cable bridges. Not much time for socializing thought the young man.

When summer rolled around Tommy had a fairly good idea how he would build his bridge. Tommy had discussed his plans with his parents. They of course thought it was a good idea but with no money to pay for materials they had tried to talk him out of the plan. Mr. Evans pointed out that the job was too big for a boy with chores and other activities in his schedule. The task would be insurmountable. All their protestations came to naught, because Tommy stuck to his resolve.

Tommy asked his dad if he could try to get a part time job at the mill.

"That would be fine," his dad said." But, you must not neglect your chores. You know that we are having a difficult time making ends meet on the farm. Your mother needs to spend time with your little sister Martha. Martha will be going to school next year, and then Mother can help out by finding a part time job in town but not before."

"I can do it all dad" replied Tommy with shear energy in his voice.

"I want to make the bridge for Martha and me so we will not be required to stay at the McPeaks."

Tommy knew that was not the only reason, but he felt that his other reason would not aid his case. Wee could have his room back. He was now free to find work at the mill for the summer. He got the job because Old Mr. Castle's grandson owned the mill and was aware of the Evans' son competence and dexterity. The grandson was also Casey's Dad. Tommy was to work three days a week helping in the lumber yard. It was hard and hot work, but Tommy never wavered in his resolve and his vision of success.

He saw Casey several times, and one day she stopped and talked to him. He was tongue tied at first because of her breathless beauty. A girl with honey colored hair. Her eyes were a deep and mysterious cobalt. Her lips spoke volumes without uttering a word. They were full and reminded Tommy of a heart. Casey was bright and gregarious. An intelligent forehead completed Tommy's close-up assessment of his friend. She began to ask about his requests for discarded slats as well as other wood requirements. Tommy had asked Mr. Castle if he could have any scraps of lumber for a project at home. Her dad must have mentioned it to Casey.

"I have decided to make a foot bridge across old Stony Creek so I can get back home when the creek rises above the wheels of our farm tractor, when the spring snow thaws bring flooding."

Casey became very interested in the project and eventually asked Tommy whether she could help in any way.

Tommy was flabbergasted at her interest in something he was going to do. Her eyes sparkled when he detailed the plan to her. For a time Tommy forgot his nervousness and talked so long Mr. Castle had to tell Casey not to bother Tommy as he has work to do. As Casey left she cast a bouquet of melodic words over her beautiful shoulder.

"Don't forget me and keep me informed as to your progress."

Tommy worked hard that summer gathering all the supplies he would need for the bridge. He had been promised some discarded cable from one of the working coal mines in area. His Dad allowed him to use the farm tractor and hay wagon to fetch the cable from the mines. Tommy made several trips, and some miners helped him load the cable. Dad helped with the unloading.

Casey rode her bike several times that summer going out towards Tommy's place and always brought something for the bridge and a little snack besides. She helped with cutting of the slats that would be the floor. Casey was a deep, beautiful well of encouragement. She told Tommy that she could see the bridge finished in her mind's eye. That gave the boy more energy to work towards that goal. He was working at the mill as well as completing his chores on the farm and with energy left over he toiled with the bridge in the night if needed. His parents began to have concerns about Tommy over doing his project. But, Tommy wanted to finish before winter set in.

Stringing the cable was the hardest part. The cable was heavy, and it took all the farm tractor had to pull the cable across the creek. The two top cables were the lightest and thinnest. The bottom cables were heaviest and harder to work with. This part was finished by the fall. Now the planks had to be secured to the bottom cables and rope between the upper and lower cables. Casey came out and helped Tommy with detail work of interlocking floor boards.

Back in school and no longer working at the mill Tommy wanted to spend as much time as possible to complete the bridge. His visions of having to stay at the McPeaks drove him on.

One night as Tommy worked late trying to beat the cold blasts of winter he fell through the cable at a point about twelve feet above the stream. The rocks bruised his back and hurt his spine.

When he straggled in the house, his Mother was shocked but not surprised.

"I just knew something like this would happen. I think we should call the doctor for you for we don't know for certain how badly you hurt yourself."

Mr. Evans concurred. The doctor came and patched up Tommy who was ordered to stay in bed for several days. Back at school Casey heard about Tommy's set-back. She came out to visit Tommy. They talked about school but always came back to the bridge. It was a delightful time for both of them as they encouraged each other and spoke of the future.

"I guess I'll not get the bridge done this year" said Tommy.

"I can come out on Saturdays to work if you tell me what to do," stated the girl of Tommy's dreams.

"I can't let you do that because the span now appears more dangerous than I imagined."

"Let's wait a few days and we can once again work together. I can be up and around in a few days. I hope those days will not matter in the whole scheme of things."

Casey was very agreeable to this plan and said so.

"I like working with you Tommy. You are so clever as well as unafraid to have a vision larger than yourself. Most of the boys in school think only about small things with no real significance. Your plan solves a dilemma for your family and friends."

Tommy almost burst at the seams. He of course, complimented Casey to the skies, enough to asked her out on a real date. She replied in the positive and after she left. Tommy did a little mental dance of Thanksgiving and joy.

God had answered his prayers. Pain starting to disappear and was no longer a problem.

The two young people continued to work on the bridge into the fall months, as well as dating from time to time. Finally, the bridge was completed to the satisfaction of Casey and Tommy. They wanted the Evans,' and the Castles to come out and be the first to officially cross the cable bridge across Stony Creek. The parents declined the offer but insisted the two young people should be the first to cross the bridge. The McPeaks had been watching all of this activity with jaundiced eye.

"It won't work" was the favorite comment from the McPeaks. Girlie frowned at the crew of two all summer and murmured something about "show-offs." Wee was sad because apple candles and lavender sprigs probably were not forthcoming.

On a cold but sunny day in December a small group of friends and family gathered at the bridge to watch Casey, and Tommy cross the span with satisfaction and joy. Holding hands they proceeded slowly, enjoying every second of the victory. Tommy forgot any aches and pains and only radiated in the presence of his lovely and talented friend. The bridge swayed a little but not Tommy or Casey, they held on to each other tight. When the crossing was completed and the crowd vigorously applauded the others took turns crossing the bridge.

The two teenagers held hands and watched the joyous scene before them unfold.

Tommy leaned over and whispered to Casey

"Would you be my very special friend"

"Of Course, Tommy, I would be proud to be your girlfriend."

Tommy thought and now knew that there is more than one kind of bridge in this world. Vision, tenacity, and dedicated work would prove the crossings needed in life. Casey and Tommy were friends and very much more, for the rest of their lives, because of a little old stream that needed crossing. Years later as proud parents the two bridge builders watched as their own children crossed that bridge. They were thankful the way things turned out.

Martha was thankful too.

CHARLEY'S SHOES

C HARLIE LIKED TO STROLL ACROSS the railroad tracks to the little city park that bordered the tracks. His summer vacation had just started, and he was able to have some free time to roam the park each afternoon after chores. He was a quiet boy. A product of hard working parents and a family of four. His ma, pa, and little sister Abigail made up the center of his universe. Although a boy of ten certainly had better things to do besides hang around home on a nice summer day.

Charlie was an average boy according to everything he could discover. Light brown hair that was unruly. Medium height and build. Some-what clumsy but with a wide and intelligent smile. Adults always said he would grow up someday and become a man. But that was to Charlie a distant event. Charlie had few friends but loved to be with grown ups, and he loved to read books. Some might call Charlie a loner, but he never felt alone. Going to the park was a liberating exercise to be around people but not have to get involved.

Arriving at the park, he was surprised that none of his acquaintances were in sight, only some old people on benches and playing games on the picnic tables. He didn't mind because old people minded their own business and only gave Charlie an occasional greeting. Charlie wasn't sure what he was looking for, but something always turned up. The park was his springboard for adventure, both actual and imaginary.

Charlie wasn't certain what the speck was. He squinted his eyes trying to brig it into focus. It laid a good way off, and he would have to walk a lot to get a better view. Opening his eyes to normal, he began the trek down the hill and across the field in the park. His curiosity was very strong, being a boy of 10. The walk was not strenuous or difficult because of his constant eying the object in question. He began to realize what the object was and slowed his walk knowing now it was not anything of value to a 10-year-old boy. Charlie bent down to pick it up to examine his most recent find.

The item before him was a practical, interesting shoe. It looked new as Charlie read the insert inside the shoe. It looked like that expensive suede leather rich people had. The bottoms were thick and made with cleats in the soles for a better grip. It certainly was something of value. It was a substantial shoe that anyone would want for their very own.

Charlie had only one pair of shoes to call his own. Not counting his old and badly worn 'little Abner shoes.' The pair he had on was his only good pair and they would have to last him the rest of the year. Being a poor boy in times of war and shoe rationing he was charged with caring for his one pair of shoes to last at least a year before his family could afford and have a war ration stamp for another pair for him. By that time, the old shoes would have worn out with cardboard soles and heels worn off on one side. On Sundays, he would clean up and polish his everyday shoes to go to church. This found shoe was the best shoe he had ever seen. The uppers were made of leather, smooth and brown. The soles were a type of composite with a rubber heel. It appeared to be brand-new. The shoe looked as though it would fit his foot so he sat down and pulled the shoe over his thin sock. It fit. This could be my shoe, thought Charlie. If only I could find the other shoe, I would be the proud owner of two pairs of shoes at one time.

Charlie looked all around trying to see whether anyone was watching or coming to reclaim his wonderful find. Seeing that no one in the area was looking his way or having the appearance of walking about on one shoe, he began to guiltily hide his new treasure. His conscience told him it was not necessary to conceal it but to hold it out in plain sight so if anyone saw it they could claim it. Placing the shoe under his arm, he slowly started home. The shoe felt hot and ten times bigger as it nestled under his arm. Holding his breath Charlie continued walking towards his home. Once there he would need a good explanation about his having in his possession three shoes when he only owned two.

His imagination started to run wild, with all kinds of scenarios on how the one shoe was found by him in the park. A mother bought shoes for her son and on the way home through the park she had inadvertently dropped and lost one shoe. If that were the case, she would be looking for that lost shoe. Knowing his mother would think along those lines, he had better return and wait for some mother looking for the lost shoe. No! Maybe some rich boy had too many shoes and thought he would just throw one away. No! That won't work, thought Charlie. With new doubts and concerns, Charlie returned to the park to monitor anyone exhibiting unusual behavior or a shoe-searching individual.

While waiting for new developments, Charlie made an intense search of the area looking for another shoe that matched his found shoe. He looked along the creek near the park and close to where he found the shoe. He found candy and gum wrappers as well as other kinds of trash but no shoe. Charlie gave up this exercise in futility. After about an hour he remembered he should be home at this time helping his mother prepare supper. With one final look all around the park, he left the area with a heavy heart. Not finding the mate to this shoe filled his head with many more questions that couldn't be answered.

Charlie also knew he would have to tell his parents about his find and listen to their instructions about the matter. Maybe they would let him keep it for his very own. Maybe his folks could buy just one shoe that would match his found shoe. MAYBE. Maybe he would have to take it to the police station with his story of discovery. The police might bawl him out for finding the shoe. Charlie wondered what the penalty was for finding a shoe and not telling anyone. This thought became uppermost in his thoughts as he neared home, now with the shoe hiding under his shirt.

Arriving in his kitchen, he was met by his mother making supper. Being so busy, she didn't seem to notice his new shoe under his shirt.

"Mom, what should someone do if they found a shoe or a hat that was just lying around the park."

"Try to find the owner to return it to them."

Charlie just knew the answer before asking it.

"Mom, suppose you couldn't find the owner, then what should you do?"

"I really don't know, but I guess one could put an ad in the paper."

"Ah Mom that would take money."

"What did you find, Charlie?"

"Just an old shoe."

"Charlie, if it is old, throw it away. If it is new, try to ask around if anyone has lost a shoe. Now help me with these potatoes"

"OK Mom. I just want go to my room for a second to do something."

"Charles, let me see the shoe. Before you hide it in your room."

Charlie could never figure out how moms knew about stuff without seeing the stuff. His mom had eyes in the back of her head, with a connection to his mind that permitted her to know everything he was thinking. There was just no sense in lying or keeping a secret, thought Charlie as he produced the shoe for his mom's inspection.

"Why, Charlie this shoe is new. You must make every effort to locate its rightful owner just as soon as possible. Keep it clean and start tomorrow to find whoever it belongs to.

They must be worried about the lost shoe and are frantically looking for it. Put it away and help me with supper."

Charlie had to repeat everything to his dad that night with comments scattered though the inquisition by his sister. He knew she was going to blab it to everybody she knew.

In the morning, Charlie started right after breakfast to find the owner of the found shoe. He left the shoe in his room so that he could better reconnoiter about the park for a person looking for a shoe.

The day was wonderful and gave Charlie a feeling of happiness because he was on a righteous quest. The grass was very green, and the sky filled with white fluffy clouds. The park was not very busy this early in the morning so Charlie sat down on one of the benches to wait. He wasn't sure of what he would do if someone were spied looking everywhere for a shoe, but he was willing to do the right thing.

The morning wore on with the usual inflow of retirees and new mothers giving their babies the fresh air treatment. Finally, Charlie got up and began a new search along the little creek in the park, hoping to find the mate to his new shoe. Upon returning from his little futile trek, he noticed a boy had occupied his previous waiting bench. The boy was his age and was accompanied with a pair of crutches. The boy might be a good source of information, thought Charlie, so he ambled over.

"Hi! My name is Charlie. Do you come here often?"

The boy looked up at Charlie with a look of surprise. The boy was Charlie's age and had dark hair. He had a very intelligent forehead with big brown eyes. Nice clothes with a hat to match gave the youngster an air of wealth. Beside him were two very nice crutches. Looking further Charlie noticed that the boy had only one foot. He felt sorry for the lad.

"My name is Boxer, and I am sort of new to this area having moved here from Capital City."

"What happened to your foot, and is Boxer your real name?" Blurted Charlie.

"Yes my name is boxer because my dad was in the Navy and as a boxer won a lot of matches so he wanted his son to become a boxer also. I lost my foot in a car accident a while ago."

"Have you seen anyone who might have lost a shoe here in the park?"

"What did it look like?" Replied Boxer.

"It was brown and very new with composition cleats for a sole."

"Oh that was mine," said Boxer.

"Did your lose it?"

"No, I threw it away with another old shoe of mine down towards the creek; in hopes that the water would carry them away. Have you found them?"

"I found the new one. Do you want it back?"

"Nah. Let me explain. My mom bought me a new pair of shoes, and I came to the park to put on one shoe and throw the old one away along with the new one that I can't use. Do you see?"

"Does that mean I can keep the new shoe I found?"

"Sure, I have no use for it with only one foot needing to be shod."

Charlie and Boxer talked for hours that day. In fact, all summer. Charlie and Boxer spent the days doing things together. They went to the mall and along the creek. They used the park with its many recreational amusements. No skate boarding or strenuous activities. Charlie helped Boxer in his movements with the crutches. They even walked the railroad tracks. They put Boxer's pennies on the rail, and waited for a train to go by thereby flattening that copper penny to a fine flat novelty.

They spent so much time together Charlie's folks became concerned because the relationship was becoming too intense. When they questioned Charlie, about how much time the boys spent together Charlie assured them he was having a wonderful time with his one footed friend by helping Boxer through his handicapped period. Boxer was an engaging boy with a wit and humor that Charlie had never seen in anyone before. His knowledge of sports and travel were amazing. The boy had a constant smile and intelligent forehead with large inquisitive brown eyes. Boxer always seemed to be positive even with his disability. People just seemed to be drawn to Boxer for comments or answers. Boxer incorporated all the traits that Charlie longed for. Boxer never once criticized or berated Charlie for having two good feet. It was understood that they were great friends that would likely last a lifetime.

Unknown to anyone was Charlie's desire to become more like Boxer. Everyday Charlie would ache because his friend seemed so alone in his handicapped position. He began to think that if he were handicapped too he would understand the feelings and difficulties that faced boxer. He began to think if he had one foot gone, they would be alike.

This youthful fantasy began to take a crooked course when Charlie began to imagine what it would be like if he had only one foot. When out of sight of any prying eyes Charlie would limp with an old tree branch for a crutch. It would have been too painful for anyone to see the young boy limping down the path to home and observe the difficulty Charlie faced when crossing the railroad tracks.

Charlie spent a lot of time in his mind turning over all the difficulties he had noticed Boxer having with the one-foot handicap. He placed himself in the same situations and dreamed of the camaraderie he would have with his friend, Boxer. His new one shoe would be all he needed. He also felt the warmth that pity would give him as family and friends saw his new condition. This imagining finally came to a climax one day when coming home from the park and a day of satisfaction with the company of Boxer.

Charlie looked at the railroad track and began to formulate a plan. If he lay down by the track with just one foot on the rail, the equalizing would only take a second. He would have to make sure he was visible to others for the run to the hospital. He knew it was a crazy plan, but his desire to be like Boxer was overwhelming.

Making sure he was out of sight at this location Charlie began to set his plan in motion. He wanted to see how laying down beside the railroad track felt as he placed one foot on the rail for a moment. It felt stupid, but the desire to be like Boxer filled his mind with images of completeness. Pulling his leg back off the track, he knew he would have to get closer to the railroad crossing so that someone would see him to call the ambulances and care for him on the scene.

Charlie walked towards the intersection and decided the spot that would be appropriate for his final act of love and loyalty. When all of the logistics were finalized in his mind, he thought it prudent to wait until tomorrow to fulfill his scheme.

All of the ramifications of his proposed action began to tumble around Charlie's mind until it just seemed to be a jumble of 'what ifs' and 'supposes.' He must not tell anyone, and he must act as though everything were normal. His mother did ask whether he felt all right or did he feel sick. Mom's had the most sensitive of feelers for trouble that Charlie ever encountered. Charlie stood steadfast in his declaration that, "Everything is all right." When Charlie went to bed early, that must have been a clue for mom because she came into his room and tried to extract from him any possible troubles he might be facing. Charlie gave out many declarations of normalcy. It was hard to convince mom, but she finally left with a small sense of assurance.

Charlie didn't sleep very well that night with dreams of trains and crutches. Such as weird things like the train stopping just before contact and the crutches chasing him and crying, "counterfeit." The night eventually wore on to morning and a sunny day.

"What a day to get things done," thought Charlie as he was dressing in great anticipation of the day's activities.

As always, mom had a number of chores for him before he ventured out in the big world. Making merry as he finished his chores he was certain that his mom had no thought of his intention that day. Charlie left his house and felt his foot for the first time, and it was good. Walking past the railroad intersection Charlie spied the spot of his sacrifice with some sense of satisfaction. "But not this morning," Charlie said out loud to no one in particular. He would find Boxer and divulge his plan to his best friend.

When entering the park Charlie didn't see Boxer and his heart almost stopped for fear he wouldn't come today to explore with Boxer. Charlie sat on a bench and waited with feelings too heavy to understand. 'What if Boxer didn't come today to share in my great adventure,' thought Charlie. Just as resolve and determination was at its lowest, Charlie looked up to see Boxer exiting his parent's car.

Boxer came on his crutches with a bounding agility Charlie had never seen before. With a hop and skip of handicapped proportions, Boxer landed next to Charlie with a smile that was as big as a sunrise. His whole being was one of joy and resembled a person full of bees and frogs, overflowing to affect even Charlie in his somber mood.

"Guess what," Boxer ejaculated. But before Charlie could attempt an answer Boxer continued.

"I am going to get a new foot in the form of a prosthesis that will permit me to walk and run with you and everyone else. What do you think of that?"

Charlie was so taken back that for a second he could not speak. Finally, he said.

"That's great boxer. When is this going to happen?"

"I am going to get fitted tomorrow, and they expect me to be hopping around in a few weeks. I have to go now as my parents are waiting. I just had to come and tell you myself about the good news. You are my best friend now. I knew you would be just as thrilled as I am because we are so much alike. I will give you this brown shoe when I no longer need it."

Charlie swallowed hard and realized his little scheme, and sacrifice would no longer be of any use. He had mixed emotions as the news permeated to his very inner being for examination and revision. Waving goodbye to his friend, Charlie turned for home. With both an exalted feeling of relief as well as a sadness of failing, Charlie walked by the designated rail track.

With a great leap of joy and happiness, Charlie was filled with the knowledge he had not done a stupid thing. The thought of grief and sadness his parents would have felt, overcame him with tears and laughter as he headed back to where he was loved and appreciated just as he was. "No need to be like someone else," he mumbled to himself. He vowed to tell no one as this was to be his secret for life. All the way home, he mulled over the events of the last two days and as he entered his house, he smelled the good cooking of his mom. Her smile was enough to wash away every foolish thought he might have had. Charlie stood on one foot as his mom finished her baking. Maybe it was all a dream thought Charlie as he tasted some apple pie his mom proffered. Soon he would have another pair of shoes so his three would turn into four. A wonderful thing to have two pairs of shoes. What a wonderful thing to be patient as well as friendly. It was wise to wait and think things through for the Lord oft-times intervened to help one to see things correctly/. Charlie was very happy for Boxer and himself. Now he wondered if he would ever meet a three-legged man.

The End

ARLO BUDGE'S MALADY

WHEN I WAS JUST A tad of a boy, my best friend was Arlo Budge. He wasn't what you would call a "keeper" but we liked each other. With him by my side, I always looked good. He had big ears that some called elephantine. He had buckteeth, freckles, and a pug nose that would please a prizefighter. He had the bristling hair of a marine sergeant. In addition, it was ruby red to boot. With all of these advantages, Arlo became a real scrapper. The two of us could lick any three bullies on the school ground. One by one or all at once. We did everything together, school, camping, fishing, fighting and just lolly gagging, while skipping stones on forbidden waters. We took long hikes and sneaked over to Featherstone's pond. Old man Featherstone owned the pond and the little general store and filling station in town. He was the town grump.

The new fangled gas pumps were a joy to behold. Mr. Featherstone or his helper

Malcolm would pump the handle to make the gasoline fill the top glass cylinder. When full to the exact mark on the glass chamber he would put out the fuel hose into the customer's gas tank and permit the measured fluid to drop into the car's tank. It was a sight to take away your breath. Gravity doing all the final work.

Mr. Featherstone had placed all kinds of signs around his pond for the edification of young boys. No swimming, no fishing, no ice skating, no frog gigging and somewhere there had to be one that said "No stone skipping" but we had not found it. We got around all these signs of instructions and guidelines by approaching the pond by backing up carefully until we reached its bank. At that point, we saw only the backs of some sign placards that didn't say anything and were blank. They all had shotgun splatter run through them anyhow.

One day we were going down to the pond to gig some frogs to please our Dads' penchant for seafood. I had my trusty steel giger while Arlo had a slick wooden stick he had made just for gigging. Arlo was very clever.

We were in fine spirits going down the road, as young boys are wont to do. We whistled and hummed a tune or two. We chucked a few stones for practice at some giant stalky dandelions. The road we took to the pond led out of town. Leaving town always made us feel good. The stress and strains of everyday life just melted away as we left and envisioned our amusements of the day ahead. It was a warm and beautiful summer day, fit for kings.

On our summer errand of joy and freedom, we saw a girl coming our way. We both recognized her as sassy Charlie. She went to our school and was even in our class. The school only had three rooms. One was for the little ones, one for the middle-ones, and the last class was for the older-ones. Arlo, this girl, and I were in the 'older-ones' class. Her name was Charlotte Arlene Hoggstett, but we all called her Charlie. She came straight for us with her bright eyes and curly hair bouncing in the summer breezes. We could tell she was full of some kind of mischief because of her skipping advance. A plain girl with no redeeming features. It was as though a wind of affliction were coming straight for us. Mean, close set eyes and a piggy nose was about to speak.

I held my breath because I had seen this grotesque creature in action before. Arlo only stiffened to a pugnacious pose.

"Going to the pond, aren't you?" Charlie spoke with a singsong in her voice while tilting her tousled head.

With her pouty lips, she declared she was going to tell Mr. Featherstone that we were going to go to his pond, disrupt its calm, and hurt its inhabitants.

Arlo raised his stick as though he might knock some sense in that addled, odious brain of hers.

"No! No! Arlo, don't strike down the fountain of truth and justice."

Arlo lowered his stick as Charlie straightened up from her expected blow.

"I'm gonna tell your ma, Arlo Budge."

"Can't you see, Arlo, that we are walking in the path of criminals and malcontents on this road to Featherstone's pond. We must bemoan our intents and return to our rooms for repentance and await further instructions from Miss Charlotte Arlene hog's breathe." (her last name was really Hoggstett)

"All right Mr. Smarty pants, I'm going to tell your ma too, all about your name calling and such. If you hadn't been so hateful I was going to ask whether I could come along and skip stones with you and Arlo, but not now."

Arlo and I looked at this fluffy dressed female with a clean face and pink hands with a certain degree of disgust. For a moment, she seemed to be like a bird without feathers, unable to fly.

"No way, you'd just get in the way and get your clothes dirty and tell your mom we did it and we'd get in trouble. You'd tell all of our friends in school that we left you to the ravages of wolves and bears so they would feel sorry for you."

With a turned up nose and sniff of disgust, Charlie left our sweet selves with her nose still held high in the air. She could drown in a rainstorm like that. I had a feeling that Charlotte Arlene Hoggstett had a secret hankering for Arlo. You may ask why? After all Charlotte Arlene Hoggstett was no prize pig herself.

This interlude left us to reminisce about times gone by.

"I remember when girls left us alone."

"I remember when we didn't have any driving machines in town"

"I remember when I built my first crystal radio."

I remember when the road in town was only gravel"

On and on it went as though two old salts were trying to relive their storybook youth on the sea.

Arlo punched the air with a delightful kernel of reminiscing. "Remember that time I missed school and you came to my house at lunchtime to inquire about my well being?"

"I sure do, Arlo you didn't come out so I met your ma on the front porch. When I asked about your absence from school, she smiled with that all knowing smiles moms always have and said you missed school because you had the Slobbering Spittles. She was uncertain how long your convalescing would be. I returned to school for afternoon classes wondering what the Slobbering Spittle's were, but I daren't ask anyone. I had had the Colly Wobbles of the Diaphragm once when I ate too many green apples and some rhubarb pie. But this malady of yours was new to me. It seems as though you can get sick awful easy like. Well, after school I came back to your house to find you sitting on the front porch with your Mom's shawl over your shoulders as if you were convalescing at the old folks home. Your mom had asked that no one should approach you on the front porch because of your terrible malady, therefore, I was to keep my distance. When I asked you how you were and what the dickens was the Slobbering Spittle's. You looked as stupefied as a bird dog bringing back a groundhog. With a look to each side of the porch, as if expecting your mom or the parson to jump out, you cupped your hands and in a confidential whisper, you told me what had happened.

Arlo picked up the reminiscing. "I think I told you the whole awful truth but for your edification, I shall again elucidate. I remember telling you that I had found my dad's jug and his pipe, still lit, behind the chicken house, where he had left them when the parson came to our house for a visit. I, being an inquisitive boy of sound mind and itching lips, had to have a slug of the squeezings and a couple of powerful draws on pa's stinky pipe, which I proceeded to do. The sky began to turn at an awful rate as my stomach turned to sailor's knots. Bile began its unwelcome rise. The whole effect, when I ran to my Mom's side was one of pure poetry of agony. Ma came close to me with a hug of certainty. I had, of course, told her everything as a son should do. She straightaway named my malady. "You have the slobbering spittle's," she said. You will have to go right to bed and stay there without any moving about or supper until you are better. So, it was, until morning, when Mom came in for her inspection. Even though I was a powerful hungry, I stood my ground. Seeing an opportunity to take off a day from school I continued with the symptoms of the Slobbering Spittle's. It worked like a charm with the exception that I had to stay in bed and not move about. After school Mom allowed me to advance to the porch but not to permit anyone to get within twenty feet of my malady."

Therefore, it was that several of us boys tried the Slobbering Spittle's routine on unsuspecting mothers. Usually it was without success. We continued on down the towards the pond.

I had mentioned that I was going to gig for plump frogs this evening for my dad's supper, Seafood for sure. Right off, Arlo had to say he would get five. I said I would get six. And so, it went until we reached twenty. That was when we ducked under the fence and began our backward walk to the pond's edge. It seemed silly to do this each time because Mr. Featherstone was too old to enforce his signs, and Malcolm was too dumb to read them. But it was part of our tradition.

The pond was deathly still at this time of day, not a bullfrog was to be heard. Yet when stumbling along its bank we saw some sunning frogs jumping in. As the evening progressed, more frogs came out. Finally, a cacophony of frog talk was heard on the other side of the pond. In his haste to gain the other bank, Arlo fell into the pond and came out dripping wet with pond grass in his hair and pond muck clear up to top of his unbuckled knickers. He was such a sight as to form in me a belly laugh of side bursting proportions. But I didn't laugh. He might try to throw me in. Instead, we decided to go home. As we walked home, with him sloshing and slushing in his wet duds and shoes, we knew we had had a wonderful day. We would go by Mr. Featherstone's store and buy some bologna for our dad's late supper. We agreed we would tell our dads it was see food. They could see it.

Arlo wondered if the Slobbering Spittle's would get him a reprieve from his sodden condition. Our moms were getting too smart for us we affirmed. Together we admitted that we didn't care. We were boys having a boyhood before it was too late to have one.

The End

BILLY BLABBERMOUTH

B ILLY BLABBERMOUTH WAS A PERIPHERAL friend of
mine. Of course, his last name was not Blabbermouth,
but we all called him that because of his constant need to talk
and dominate most conversations. I liked him because he
was different. His parents were both deep into academia. His
dad being a professor and his mother a teacher. In our day,
he was called an egghead or brain. Today the designation
would be a nerd.

Billy didn't have a bike so I let him ride mine after school
for a nickel. Not a large sum but enough for a candy bar or
a one-dip ice cream cone. My daddy always told me to get
smart by associating with smart kids, so that was what Billy
and I were doing. Billy was also very smart as well as being
full of it. I mean information. I don't know how he had all the
most recent news about the other kids and even some of the
teachers. His mouth would go a mile a minute as he blabbed
away about anything and everything. I usually didn't listen
closely because of all the adjectives and big words that made
one dizzy. Nevertheless, once in awhile I caught a key word
or two that could lead to something interesting.

Billy had the most annoying habit of talking to people
and twisting a button on their shirt or sweater. This habit
was probably the one thing he did that caused others not to
associate with Billy for very long. No one asked him why he
twisted their buttons. They just moved away from him and
chose not to allow him to speak to them again. His friends
were few and far between. However, I had a bike that he just
loved to ride it after school for only a nickel. Ice cream and
colas danced in my head as he blabbed before me this day. A
nickel well earned by me. His lips sometimes spewed forth

some spittle so I had to move back a tad away from his button twisting quirk.

Billy was thin and had dark, long eyelashes. His eyes were of that dark blue that had the effect of looking through you as he blabbed on. His nose was aquiline, and his skin very white. His hair was straight and parted on one side so that some times part of it fell over his forehead to give him a slightly Germanic appearance. His ears moved in concert with his mouth, appearing as vibrating pans that were receiving information as he blabbed. Listening to him was an agonizing sort of joyful misery. Just watching him in preparation for my accepting my hard earned nickel gave me the inner willies.

As I listened now, a few key words began to drop into my brain that triggered a sense of adventure. Words like, treasure, fortune, money, and bike ride. With these words, I developed a new sense of attention to the blabbering lips and hard blue eyes. Billy was describing an adventure of immense proportions for a young boy with a bike and body ready to go forth from humdrum and ho hum to fame and fortune.

Billy Blabbermouth was telling of a book he had read recently that told of a bank robbery in the next county that was most interesting. He went on:

"The robbers were caught, but the sacks of money were never recovered. The robbery was in Union City, but the perpetrators were caught in Capitol City without the loot. My calculations are such that they must have stashed the loot between the two cities. The cops looked, but never discovered any money. They were very ineffective in those days. This was years ago, and I feel that the money is still out there waiting to be found. I have looked at a lot of maps and aerial photos and have concluded that the cops looked on the main roads only. I found in one aerial photo of an old road between the two cities that are not on any regular map. Both crooks were captured in the south soon after the heist. Both were soon sprung by clever lawyers and were last heard of living in some island nation, never revealing any information about the bank job. I am certain the loot is still out their for us to find. My plan is for us to bike out to the next county, find this road and their hideout where the sacks are hidden. We can do it! We are clever and resourceful in all other things. This would be a piece of cake if we join together"

While he was taking a deep breath for his next verbal onslaught, I jumped in with all of the difficulties we would encounter.

"You don't have a bike and two on one is out of the question. The trip you propose is more miles than I have ever traveled on my old trusty bike. Our parents—" He cut me off

"I can take Roger's bike. Some one is always taking it or running it up the flagpole. He is so accustomed to those high jinxes he would not even bother telling his folks or the gendarmes. I will hide it in Mr. Gogley's garage next door to me. He has no car and never goes in the garage. I will take it on Friday so that we can get going on Saturday morning, early."

I saw that Billy was intense and determined to go through with this ill-advised plan. I finally heard myself say, "OK. Let's do it."

The next day or two we talked about the plan as well as being very clandestine in our conversations. When Friday rolled around Billy very carefully took Roger's bike and hid it in Mr. Gogley's garage as planned. Roger just shook his head, when after school he noticed the bike missing. He went home on shanks ponies without a word of alarm, just as planned.

The next morning on Saturday, we both left early after giving plausible but flimsy excuses to inquisitive parents. The ride out of town was full of excitement and anticipation. When safely in the country we stopped and compared notes on supplies etc. I had brought some tools for any mechanical contingencies. We each brought water and food for the days long trek. After examining the food supply, we each had a candy bar for the early morning ride of our life.

It was not too hard to follow the map that Billy had brought. He was meticulous about lines and squiggles on the paper he had prepared as the map. We folded it and unfolded it so many times it began to want to come apart at the seams. It was coming apart when we finally arrived at the place where Billy insisted that the regular road met the abandoned road. All I saw was a fence and a lot of brush. Getting off of our bikes, Billy got on his knees to examine the ground at the place of possible entry. After a period of time, while I was eating another candy treat, Billy gave out an exclamation of success.

"Here it is. Just as I had anticipated. We will have to take the bikes over the fence and hide them and then go on foot the rest of the way. It won't be long now."

Billy was so ecstatic with verbiage and with sputtering of such proportions he actually quivered with excitement.

We pulled our bikes over the fence and soon had them concealed from any prying eyes in the vicinity. The old road was barely visible even with youthful eyes and frequent examinations by bending the back close to the ground. Our progress was slow but certain. The map was not so important now, so Billy let me carry it as he led the way through the grasses and scrub.

The day was warm but not hot, but our exertions began to produce perspiration and discomfort because of our coats. We both removed our jackets for a more comfortable saunter. Overhead was the bright sky as the white clouds moved to give shade and sunlight in alternate pauses. We had slowed considerable to not bypass the path to a yet invisible cabin. Billy had really slowed as he exclaimed.

"We are close; very close. I can almost smell the money we will soon possess. Keep a lookout for any signs of an old path that will lead us to our fortune."

In only minutes we had located what appeared to be an over grown path. With mumbling and sputtering we both began to move bent over and quickly up the faint pathway looking for a cabin or any structure. We were soon rewarded with the appearing of an old rustic cabin of ancient construction, leaning like a crooked smile. Billy was ready to explode with exclamations and declarations of victory. He looked like a boy without any sense or caution. Billy stood up and with a whoop and holler of gargantuan proportions, he began to run with abandon towards the old rickety structure. It appeared as an old hunting cabin with no windows but shutters covering the window openings. The roof was made with cedar shakes, now turning to gray powder. The siding was curled and coming away from the cabin's structure. Off to one side was an ancient water pump, rusted to look like a frozen lump. Weeds had grown to waist high, and the whole structure seemed to sag with age and neglect.

Billy didn't care. He viewed the shack as a bank vault or a castle with unlimited wealth. The front door was jammed tight because of the structures leaning condition. However, with boyish glee, he attacked the nearest window opening and tore off its sagging shutter. With pent up enthusiasm, Billy jumped up and over the opening, even after my loud protestations and cautions. I ran to the window just as Billy emitted a loud cry of pain and surprise. Looking into the opening, I saw the cause for the awful verbal ruckus coming from one hurting and surprised Billy Blabbermouth.

Billy was knee deep with his right leg in a broken floor that resented his 100 pounds of jumping flesh. After he leaped through the window, the boards gave way in such a manner as to wedge his one thigh with jagged splinters waiting for any sudden upward movement. If the thigh were raised the splintered board would dig deeper into his flesh. One broken board on each side of his exposed upper leg prevented his freedom. He couldn't push down for relief because his knee was set against the ground, below the floorboards. His moans of pain and failure were bittersweet sounds to my ears. He deserved his predicament. He stopped long enough to shout that the two canvas moneybags were in the cabin's corner.

The room was small and furnished only with a rickety table and a rocking chair. On the far wall was a lopsided empty cupboard with only the remains of nesting material from the ever-present mice. The two canvas bags were leaning in a corner, looking very sad with holes in several places were mice had probably found nesting material of the costliest kind.

Billy's yips and yells for me to do something caused me to climb into the room with care and agility through the narrow wind Finding the cross beams for better support so that the rotten floorboards would not give way with me, I knelt by the blabbering boy for a close inspection of the situation. The boards were still wedging Billy's thigh so I just pushed down with my hand on one side to free it from the splintered ends so he could move his leg around to pull it out of the confining predicament. That was a mistake I was to remember for a long time.

With lightening like speed, Billy bounded forward towards the canvas bags and with a mighty shout of victory raised them up with one in each hand. To our surprise, the bottoms of both bags gave way as rotten or decimated cloth. The contents came tumbling out only to reveal their contents to us. Billy grabbed at the packets that had been chewed on and had turned to dusty tinder. With a loud and painful cry, Billy ejaculated his most awful revelation.

"These are not currency notes. They are only packets of cut magazines and newspapers to look like bundles of money. We have been bamboozled."

The hurt in his voice was pathetic, maybe more so than his physical misery. Billy rummaged through the sacks to see if any bundles had contained real money. I watched with my mouth open in amazement as Billy searched each disintegrating sack. He found several rolls of coins that had been in the corners of the canvas satchels. He pocketed the rolls of coins and finished his search with much muttering with words of anger and annoyance. When the awful truth became evident to both of us, it was now the time to divide the 4 rolls of coins.

Billy kept the two rolls of quarters saying he was the mastermind of the adventure and should be rewarded the two rolls of quarters at ten dollars each. He gave me the two rolls of dimes with only a comment.

"That gives us each two rolls of coins to spend and it will have to be recompense enough for our efforts this day and something to brag on. Twenty dollars for me and ten dollars for you."

I knew that it would be fruitless to argue with Billy for he was the instigator of the plan, and he would out talk me on the subject for hours if need be.

The trip home was without any incidents. But, there was a lot of mumbling and railings by Billy into the sweet autumn breezes.

When we returned home, Billy put Roger's bike back on the school ground and then we bid farewell to one another as we headed to our homes.

I put my two rolls of dimes away for safekeeping, but I found out later that Billy had spent his twenty dollars in quarters on a new bike. We never saw much of each other as we progressed in school. Billy riding his new bike so that the girls began to notice him.

The local police revealed the story about the money to us, when we finally got the courage to reveal our find of the bank money sacks. It was told to us the bank had orchestrated the holdup as a ruse to cover mammoth loses. A bank official had hired the bank robbers to pull off the job. The insurance money was used to cover the financial misconduct. Both the insurance company and bank had gone belly up in the ensuing years, so the police theorized we could keep the coins. They thanked us for the find so they could close the case.

The years went by as Billy rode his new bike, so I had no one to pay me for a bike ride anymore. We went our separate ways, and Billy ended up opening a bike sale and repair shop. I had on the other hand reached college age and opened my 2 rolls of dimes to find they were uncirculated 1931D dimes that had become very valuable. It was enough to send me to college. The last I heard of Billy Glabberhut (his real name) he was selling bikes and blabbing to folks to buy a bike while twisting buttons off the prospective buyer's shirts.

The End

POPPY'S SECRET

POPPY LIVED IN A SMALL village in the Midwest. Mt. Mildew was small by any standard. The people were all very conservative and industrious. Most folks kept to themselves and usually minded their own business. Poppy loved the little town.

Poppy was old. So old no one knew how old. When anyone tried to find out about his birth they were always stymied by events like the courthouse fire of 1933 or the flooded library of 1937. Even the weekly newspaper had only begun in 1947. The hospital had moved so many times all their records were someplace else. The school was consolidated in 1954 and all the old records were left in the old school that burned down 2 years later. Even the churches had no record of his membership. The oldest sages in town remembered Poppy as being old when they were just youngsters looking at him as an ancient relic. No one knew how he became known as Poppy. It was too long ago.

Poppy walked the streets of the town with his burlap gunnysack. When he went shopping, he would place his purchases in the sack and have the clerk ring up the sale and replace the merchandise in the sack. It was the same with groceries, hardware, clothing, or shoes. They eventually all went into the sack. Poppy visited all the stores as well as his favorite establishments which were the library, the post office, and the bank. Every one knew his name and greeted him with respect. All questions were answered by just a few syllables. "Yes' and 'no' were heard the most. He was most polite but had no hankering to extend the conversation beyond a few words to most folks. He just walked away as though it was an inquisition.

Everyone knew he was retired but from what was not known. Some speculated he had been in the army; others thought maybe a police career had been in his past. Several wags in town opined that he was a professor. They based it upon his short replies and his desire to be left alone, even though it was known he was a good listener when convenient for him.

"Wouldn't you be like that after years of teaching ungrateful and undisciplined kids?" They would offer as a reason for his aloofness if he had been a professor. All of his bearing radiated that a secret was harbored in those old washed out blue eyes.

Any one could at a distance, recognize that the form in their view was Poppy. He usually wore his giant khaki long coat, except in the summer. (Maybe he was cold because of poor circulation.) His gait was sure but had more of a slide than a stride as he moved along the street, slightly bent over. From behind one could see his gray hair fluffed up under his watch cap. His shoes were worn on one side of each shoe, giving his walk a bowed legged effect. With all of these defects, you could still tell the man had bearing and dignity.

It is thought that someone said years ago that Poppy had a secret. He just looked as though he harbored a secret they said. The rumor was handed down from parent to child until that rumor persisted to this day. This idea was fortified by several break-ins at Poppy's house, in the poorer section of town. The burglars were caught and confirmed they found nothing of value. This scenario was certainly not Poppy's secret.

Poppy's house was one of the oldest houses in town. It was believed that it was once a trader's house where homesteaders would bring furs and crops to town, receiving staples, and cash in trade. It was this dubious maxim that caused many to believe Poppy had a cache in the old house. The house was made of great stone blocks, except the addition on the back. The addition contained the kitchen, an eating area, and commode and heating unit. The front, made of stone was square; one storied and contained Poppy's bedroom and sitting room. It was a cute and sturdy house painted white with shutters in front. The back yard was spacious with a detached building that might have been a garage. A grape arbor and garden competed the large lot.

In the summer, Poppy grew a large garden. On summer days, one could see Poppy pushing an old baby buggy down the streets in town, selling his produce. His vegetables were the most desirable produce in the county. Was that Poppy's secret? How did he grow such luscious fruit and vegetables when others usually failed? When other gardens dried up or were bugged to death, Poppy had a bumper crop. All of the green thumbs in town itched to know Poppy's puzzling success. When asked about his gardening techniques he was quick to answer all questions and even gave advice, so that surely wasn't his secret. Composting was his answer to their inquiries. Tobacco juice to kill al the offending bugs. Nothing special here.

Poppy had a family. He did confide to some oldsters in town that he had a daughter and wife that left town many years ago, never to be heard from again. People tried to get Poppy to divulge more about his family but Poppy was tight lipped about any family. Was the fact that one of his family had become very famous and Poppy was too proud to admit it? Was that Poppy's secret?

Poppy was very gregarious when in a talkative mood. He could be seen on good days talking to some folks for hours when it suited his purpose.

Constable Moon Pierson, the local gendarme, was one that whiled a-way many hours with Poppy but found that he was unable to extract any real information from the old man.

"Poppy is well versed in the law but I don't think he was ever a policeman or a lawyer," Moon said.

Miss Frost was also a favorite of Poppy; She was the local schoolteacher of ancient origins. She taught kids, their parents, and even some grandparents but she never remembered teaching Poppy or any of his family. Poppy would catch her coming out of the school and invite her to have tea with him at Miss Lipman's teahouse. They would sit for hours as Miss Frost talked the ears off of Poppy. Was Poppy trying to grasp things, with his notebook in hand. that helped his mind as Miss Frost chattered away? Was that Poppy's secret?

Barney Cash, the local banker, was also a favorite of Poppy. Barney could talk your arm off as well as bending an ear to the breaking point. Barney was great to wave his arms around almost hitting Poppy, as the conversation got very intense. As much time as Barney spent talking to Poppy, it was supposed, Poppy had loads of money. Was that Poppy's secret?

Sammy Stamp, the local postmaster was also on the selected list of privileged conversationalists. Sammy would come out from behind the counter to instruct Poppy about postal rates when sending off parcels. They would talk for great lengths of time, about the weather, about hunting and gardening, etc. It was hard to get even a penny postcard when those two were at it.

It was presumed that Poppy was not a very religious man. He attended Church but never went into the sanctuaries. On most any Sunday, you could find Poppy sitting on the front steps at various Churches. One Sunday it would be at the Methodist Church and the next Sunday, it would be the Baptist Church and so on. Only when the weather was inclement, did Poppy finally venture into the vestibules after the service began to keep out of the rain or snow. You could crane your neck and see him with his little notebook trying to keep warm and dry. When Church was over Poppy was gone before anyone could greet him before rushing out to their Sunday fried chicken. Once in awhile he would talk to a preacher but never on Sunday. Preachers loved to talk about everything as well as religion. That was surely not Poppy's secret.

One day, several people began to inquire about the whereabouts of Poppy. He wasn't seen at any Church on Sunday, inside in the vestibule or out on the steps. It was mid January and the weather snowy and bitter cold. His friends in town began to compare notes about his presence anyplace on Sunday. All reports were negative. A small delegation was appointed to seek out the old fellow at his house down on Hill Avenue. Barney and Stamp as well as Moon the cop all gathered at noon to discover the old boy's situation. They approached the little white house with shutters and knocked on the door. No answer. They went around to the back of the residence and found Poppy in the snow with a snow shovel in hand. Bending down to see whether life still existed in the old man, Moon was saddened to declare the demise of Poppy.

Moon made all the arrangements for the funeral of Poppy. At the funeral home and at the gravesite burial, most of the residents of Mt. Mildew attended. Hundreds of people were milling around the cemetery on that cold snowy day as several local ministers said all the right words as Poppy was lowered into the ground. Whispers were heard everywhere. "What was his secret?" "Did he have a family?" "Where they here in the crowd?"

They town mourned for days as the courts opened his house and records to try to dispose of Poppy's estate. All in the know were bombarded with questions about Poppy's effects. Little by little, it was disclosed that Poppy was an author of many famous novels, making him a millionaire. He had written many books and was well know by his pen name, Tommy Tattler. The town folks were chagrined to discover that all of the townspeople had made it into one or more of Poppy's novels. All the names were changed but upon scrutiny, each could find their own character written in the novels of Tommy Tattler. Most were in a good light as they treated Poppy but a few were depicted as hard or bitter just as they really where. That was Poppy's secret. He had for years used the people and the events surrounding them as fodder for well-read novels. His money was for the most part, given to the town to improve all the institutions and infrastructures. Some folks cried and some laughed but they all would remember Poppy's secret, recording the town's *human well* of secrets.

LILY WHITE AND HER PASSAGE TO VICTORY

L ILY WHITE LIVED IN THE top of a mountain. She didn't really want to live there, but circumstances drove her to her mountain top retreat. She lived in a house made of cold gray stone. The mountain was also cold and gray most of the time.

The house was built by someone long ago, their name long since forgotten. This house, now her house, consisted of two very spacious rooms. The front room was fitted with an enormous fireplace, a kitchen with wood burning stove, a dining table, comfy chairs and many cabinets to store her goods. The front door was made of a heavy oak to keep out old man's wintry blasts. Two small windows were in the front wall that looked out on the mountain's splendor.

The front of the house had a long porch the length of the house. In the summer, Lilly White could sit on her porch and look out over all of the valleys below and to contemplate her dilemma.

Inside, the wall was constructed of great gray stones. Very sturdy and sound. They kept out the mountains snow and ice and other unwanted intrusions. The floors were also made of great gray stones, worn smooth by those that had inhabited this house in years past.

The other room was the bedroom, also used for study, reading, and writing. In one corner was a piano that Lily loved to play when her mood was such that it needed lifting. This room was also made with great gray flagstones all on the floor. The only difference with this room and the front room was that it was built completely inserted into the mountain. The builder had carved out the solid stone mountain to place the bedroom within the mountain itself. No regular windows or regular ceiling. The walls and ceiling were of the mountain itself. Cool but not cold to the touch. The design was such that in the winter's most severe blasts and bullying, the occupant could retreat into the bedroom and escape the terrible cold because the interior stayed nearly the same temperature all year long. Not cold and not hot, sort of an innocuous temperature.

Her house was perfect for Lily White even though she had to perform many difficult tasks. She would spend days in the summer gathering wood from the mountain slopes to keep her warm in the winter's frigid grasp.

During the waning of summer, both sidewalls of the front room as well as much of the front porch were covered with wood of all sizes and lengths. She gardened on one side of the mountain, the south, growing almost all of her sustenance. Potatoes, spinach, cabbages, beans, squash, grapes, berries, and many other eatables. Lily White canned, dried, and salted all of her food in the summer so that she would have enough food to keep her all winter. Once a year she would venture down the mountain to purchase needed supplies. Water came from a spring near-by. All in all Lily's house was snug as well as isolated from the adversities of the world.

It was a hard life but one that Lily White had chosen because of the difficulty in the valley down below. It was a long and painful story to say the least. She had no family. They all were killed in the great avalanche of many years back. Her schooling was completed in the government school down below. That's were the trouble began.

Lily White was slim and not what you would call pretty. She was small boned and petite. Her nose was small and her teeth appeared to be very white but slightly more prominent than other folks. She had slender fingers and straight blond hair that was always wisping in the wind. Her eyes of course were blue as the glacial lakes found in the valleys below.

The boys in school always called her ugly and skinny. Probably because she would not enter their contemptible games and uncouth behavior. One boy, Red Carnation, would pelt her with crab apples and stones whenever she was in close proximity. Knocking books out of her hands also was a favorite game of her antagonists.

Lily White had some friends that tried to help her but to little avail. One of her friends was Ivy Vine. Ivy would try to get Lily to throw back some apples at the boys. Ivy became very combatant as she slowly railed back at the behavior of Cactus Jack. Ivy changed so that she began to intimidate other kids in school. It was like a disease.

Cactus started bad rumors about Lily so that he looked like a big shot. Red Carnation and Cactus Jack continued to tease and intimidate Lily to the point of tears.

She once had a friend named Rose Thorn. Rose heard some of the rumors that Cactus Jack, started and she believed them. This caused Lily to loose a friend because of these terrible rumors. Rose Thorn struck Lily with poison glances and hurtful tales. It was like a disease.

Lily just would not retaliate because of her upbringing and gentle spirit. Her folks had died and left her with a house and a small residual. With these two, she was quite independent. Upon graduation, she moved up the mountain to her stone house and now lived in nearly complete solitude. A house no one else wanted.

One cold and wintry night as Lily read her bible, the Lord spoke to her heart. Lily had spent several years on the cold mountain and was beginning to desire some human companionship. While praying about this craving the Lord spoke to her heart and said she must go back down the mountain and ask for forgiveness from Cactus Jack and Red Carnation and the other friends that had caused her pain.

Of course, she began to argue that it was those mean people that needed to be forgiven. "I have not done anything wrong," she murmured.

"That's it," said the Lord, "Your thoughts are not pure."

Her heart was troubled but she continued to read the bible far into the night. During this night, she surrendered to the Lord and made peace with God by accepting his grace and salvation and forgiveness.

In the morning, she experienced a newness that she had never felt before. Everything was bright and good. She smiled and sang new songs from her heart. Her face was washed with tears of joy and relief all the daylong. Before long she made plans to return down the mountain to seek out her old tormentors and tell them that she forgave them and would they forgive her. This change of heart made the days pass with a rapidity not experienced before.

She would stay with her best friend Rose Petal. She would then go and seek out Red Carnation and Cactus Jack and testify to what had happened to her and ask for their forgiveness concerning her being so skinny and ugly. Her thoughts of revenge and bitterness towards those below were now changed. It would be a glorious time she mused, even if they hurt me again.

The big day finally came in the spring. It was a cloudless sky of brilliant blue that accompanied our Lily White down the mountain to the valley. She literally was skipping her way down the mountain trail. The crisp spring air was filled with songs of praise and thankfulness. Even the birds of the woods seemed to chime in and share her joyous descent. From time to time, she would stop and reflect on how hard it had been to climb this unfeeling mountain, even with help from her friend Rose Petal. She had been so weak and tired all the time. Going up had been an excruciating trek to avoid the taunts of others. Now she was going down in a matter of hours and not a full day as she had done on the other occasions when descending.

When she reached the village, no one had spied her as she took her meager belongings to her friend's house. Rose Petal greeted Lily White almost as soon as Lily knocked at the door. Each looked at the other in amazement. Almost in unison, they exclaimed.

"You Look so different!"

They reached out and hugged each other as long-lost friends do as well as just friends do. Tears began roll down and glisten the cheeks of the two friends as they tried to speak and tell each other about their situations.

"I got married," blurted out Rose Petal as an infant's cry broke the bubble of euphoria.

"So I hear," responded Lily.

Soon, they were telling each other all about the things that had happened in the intervening years of separation. It had been more than a year since Lily had been down in the valley.

Rose Petal had become a Christian and had helped bring Red Carnation into the Church where he got saved and changed. They married soon after hat, and had little Pink a year later. Rose, Pink and Red were very happy and involved in the little Church in the dell.

"What ever happened to Cactus Jack?" Lily asked with a lump in her throat.

"Oh he is just as mean as ever and sits on his porch all day and throws insults at everyone that goes by. His language is disgusting. He hasn't worked or taken a bath for about a year now. He has let his hair grow long and scraggly and a bushy beard of the most unkempt nature. We have tried to witness to him but have not been successful."

Rose Petal, now Rose Carnation ended this information with a long sigh. She returned to her motherly duties for little Pink Carnation.

"Red will be home later this evening and you will not recognize his new look of joy and peace."

Lily felt it necessary to relate to Rose all that had happened to her several months earlier on the mountain and what the Lord had spoken to her heart. It would now be easy to ask Red for his forgiveness, but it appeared as though the confrontation with Cactus Jack would be most prickly.

Rose said, "she and Red would pray for her as she went to Cactus to witness the Lord's goodness."

Red Came home later and the three of them had a wonderful time in the Lord. They spoke of old times only a little but lifted up the future in glowing terms and declarations. Red, of course was forgiven as well as forgave as the scriptures dictate to all those in the family of God. They stayed up late and rejoiced in the days ahead. Singing songs and quoting scripture until it became a real necessity to retire and get some sleep. They prayed Lily to reap good results when she encountered Cactus Jack.

The morning came with great expectation and joy, for this was the day that the Lord had made. After a sumptuous breakfast, Rose sent off Lily with words of encouragement and love.

Lily walked down the streets that had once been so very dear to her as a little girl. Yet some trepidation crept in when she saw the little schoolhouse and all of the taunting and teasing came flooding back.

Taking every thought captive to the obedience of Christ. She moved on down the street with even more determination and resolve. Looking ahead, she saw Cactus Jack's, house and sure enough, he was sitting on the front porch with all of the appearance that Rose and Red had told her. When she got closer, Cactus Jack leaned over the railing and began a tirade. It was as mean as anything Lily had ever heard. She was sure he didn't recognize her because the comments were of such a generic nature that could embarrass anyone to tears or anger.

She continued to approach the porch even though words of intimidation came spewing out of the mouth of Cactus.

"What do you want and who are you?" Cactus spoke with a slur as he tipped a bottle of spirits to his lips." "Go away!"

Lily came a little closer as she said. "Don't you know me? "I've come to talk to you and ask for your forgiveness"

"I don't know you and don't want to talk about forgiveness."

Cactus Jack almost stumbled on the word and his eyes began to take on a look of surprise.

"I certainly don't need to forgive anyone even though I need some forgiveness myself."

The words came out crystal clear and without any slurring as though a miracle of sobriety came over Cactus all at once.

Lily finally disclosed who she was and all about the errand, she was on. She told about her conversion on the mountain and her desire to set all things right, including being forgiven for being so skinny and ugly.

All at once Cactus stood up from the rocking chair almost upsetting it in the process.

"You are not skinny or ugly now," he said. "In fact you are beautiful, you have grown into a lovely wonderment. I can forgive you but I can not be forgiven because I have been so mean and bad."

Lily spent a long time with Cactus Jack but could not convince him of the forgiveness of God and the Life of joy and happiness ahead for him if he chose to accept Christ as his personal Lord. She eventually left to return to Rose Carnation's house exhausted but not defeated. She assured Cactus Jack she would return sometime in the future to see whether he had changed his mind.

When returning to the Carnations,' she related to both Rose and Red all that had transpired with the visit with Cactus Jack.

They spent the evening in good fellowship. Baby Pink was the center of attention until put to bed. They talked of scriptures and faith long into the night and capped off the session with prayer for Cactus and others in need.

"I hope that Ivy Vine and Rose Thorn are in the village so can I go to them also, asking for their forgiveness too," Lily White spoke with love.

"No need to go there, Lily, they both had moved from the valley and have never been heard from since," said Rose.

In the morning the talk centered on what Lily was going to do now that she had found peace and contentment, no longer needing to isolate her in a cold gray environment, far from contact with others. She wasn't certain about her next move but had promised God one more visit to Cactus before going back to the mountain.

After several days, Lily set off again to give another try to convince Cactus of his need for repentance and The New Birth. She took with her some of Rose's home made pastries to sweeten up the Cactus man. When she arrived at the porch, no one was in the rocking chair or anywhere about. When knocking on the door she heard singing coming from within. Her knocking interrupted the joyous sounds but not the sound of someone bounding down the stairs.

To her utter surprise, a young man of handsome appearance came to the door and invited her in. It was Cactus Jack, clean-shaven, washed, and combed hair and smelling of soap from head to toe. His smile was brilliant with shining white teeth. He had on a clean white shirt and blue slacks. This man was different than any Cactus Jack that Lily had even seen. His eyes were clear and his smile fetching.

"What has happened, Cactus Jack? Lily blurted out before she thought what she was saying.

"Come in Lily and sit down. I have a thousand things to tell you of the most wonderful nature. It is hard to believe, but believe I must."

Lily came in and sat down and as they shared the pastries, she had brought, Cactus Jack told her of the Lord's coming to him late at night. He had been so taken by the boldness of her earlier visit he began to search the scriptures and meditate on the WORD. Eventually God spoke to his heart and showed him his needs and condition.

"Well, after a flood of tears I came to give my life to the lord and he forgave me of my past and set me up for a future. Christ is certainly the King of second chances I am a new creature in Christ. You impressed me Lily. You are so beautiful and bubbly. I knew after your visit I wanted what ever you had found on the mountain to change you so dramatically. Would you forgive me for all the hurt and harm I caused you in the past?" Cactus could hardly get out his request before tears began to roll down his cheeks.

"Of course I will forgive you and will forget all that dark past as the Lord has also done," said Lily.

They both embraced as brother and sister in the Lord and then spent hours talking about the scriptures and what lay ahead.

. Lily stayed with her friend, Rose during the spring. During this time, she began to date Cactus Jack, which surprised everyone. In the summer, Lily declared that she had to return to her house on the mountain, but Rose and Cactus talked her out of returning to the summit of Mt. Hopelessness. Lily stayed and finally married Cactus Jack and never returned to the house in the mountain.

Lily sold the mountain retreat to a young man that was short and skinny, with large eyeglasses. He had been taunted through school and fought many a battle with bullies and cowards. Lily was glad to rid herself of the cold, gray stone house but sad that someone else would want to live there for a while. However, it would not be for long because she left her bible there when she and Cactus Jack moved her articles back down the mountain when they got married. They also prayed in each room for the Spirit of love, power, and a sound mind to prevail in that abode. Lily and Cactus Jack felt in their hearts; that due to these prayers to a loving and merciful God who desires all men to be saved and come to the knowledge of the truth, it was only a matter of time when the young man would come back down that gray and dreary mountain. Lily Jack was very certain.

The End

JACK AND THE BLUE BOX©

J ACK LIVED IN A SMALL town in a small county in a small
state. In his day, most things were small. The town
was of about twelve houses or fifteen if you counted kinfolks
that lived in some cellar houses. Jack always complained that
nothing happened in Robsnest, his little town. That was,
until the Jack found a huge box in the road outside his house.
The box was dark blue and sturdily made.

The hamlet of Robsnest got its name, according the local
wags, when some pioneers were going west. Suddenly, a storm
of blizzard proportions visited the folks in an unkindly way.
They were forced to hunker down and stay put for the winter.
With only a few provision the little group toughed out the
cold snowy winter. Eventually, the winter faded. One day
one of the half-frozen clan noticed a happening of spiritual
pleasing dimensions. She was heard shouting repeatedly, "a
robin's nest, a robin's nest, a robin's nest." This went on for a
spell until a kindly gentleman with courage and perception
put his hand across her mouth to bring peace and tranquility
back to the frozen camp. It most likely was her husband.
Spring had finally come to thaw out the little group. The
majority of the folks stayed on and made their homes in the
immediate area. Like most of us, they slurred the tale as well
as forgot its importance about the robin in question. Robin's
nest was soon contracted like so much of truth. Robsnest
was sounded out in the years following and Robsnest stuck.
Jack liked the name.

The only place of importance in his town was Mr.
Henshen's store. Mr. Henshen had built on an addition to the
front of his house to accommodate the store. It had everything
from gumboots to canned sardines. When entering the store

Mr. Henshen would appear like an apparition from behind some faded red curtains that separated the store from the house. His tall, ghostly form approached with hope in his sunken eyes. "What can I get you, boy?" The words came forth with a low rumble that nearly duplicated the sound of a coming storm. It had a sort of death rattle attached to the question. Jack gave Mr. Henshen the list with his Mother's wants. Jack wandered about the store while Mr. Henshen pulled the order together. Henshen's store sold fishing lures, cans of assorted kinds, and even a great icebox for perishable goods and fishing bait. He also would sell game the boys would shoot and bring to the store. He shared the profits equally. Mushrooms in the spring as well as greens could be brought to the store for sharing and chickens for sale when you wanted to thin your flock. Jack's dad bought a pig every year and it was fattened up all summer long with our leavings. In the fall, his dad would butcher the great beast and made sausage from all of the pig. It was the best and the most delicious sausage ever. What his mom didn't can they took to the store and Mr. Henshen sold it to folks from as far away as Whiskey Holler. And as always, He always split the profits equally. It was a time when men's honesty still was a living virtue, and a smile was more than a forced facial reflex.

Of course, Jack thought of Mr. Henshen and the store as he looked at the box on the road, with great excitement. Jack knew he would have to move it because a rider on horseback or some one in a wagon or carriage might hit it in the night with dire consequences. Jack was a quick thinker. His dad was in the hills with a lumber crew cutting trees so he could not help. Old Perky, the mule would be his only helper unless he called on Red Jack. Red Jack was his best friend along with Green Jack and Gray Jack. The four boys called themselves the cracker Jacks. (Our Jack was Blue Jack.)

The name calling all happened several years before. When the boys entered the one room schoolhouse for first year they noticed the school Marm having trouble differentiating between the four Jacks in the room. Each boy's name was really John. But before they could walk, their fathers tagged them with Jack. No one could change that. The boys, seeing the difficulty, became fast friends. They decided on their own to solve the problem. One day they gathered around an old stump in the woods just outside of their hamlet. With fox tails and chicken blood they made a pact that would keep the boys names separate. They cast lots for colors to be used in their name. They all had agreed that their respective middle names were unworthy to be used. Names like Slouson and Ferttle did not fit the boy's character. The first lot went to our Jack. He chose blue and was known from then on as Blue Jack. Each boy in succession picked colors as the lot fell to him. Red Jack came next and then Green Jack. The last lot fell and with colors such as yellow, black, pink, violet. orange not in the running for our young impetuous group, the last boy chose gray. Gray Jack. The boys wrote their respective names in chicken blood on their arms with the base of the foxtail. It was official. The adults had all tried to dissuade the boys of the color differentiation. To no avail. For the next year, the color their friends used as a code, and finally even the parents succumbed to the boys' code from then on. Teachers likewise found the code to their advantage when calling on the boys in school.

This of course brings us back to the large crate or box painted blue, with oriental writing all over the outside. The possible shipping tag had been pulled from its wire anchor when falling from its original wagon abode. The results being, no delivering addresses. Since the box was blue and apparently, fell out of the sky or freight wagon, Blue Jack was certain it belonged to him. Dad was away and Mom knew right from wrong, so he surmised by twelve-year old logic neither one of them should be told. It must be removed before dad came home for he always had an inquiring nature that amazed Blue Jack. With that in mind, he summoned

Red Jack and Green Jack to come help him move it off the road.

The boys gathered around the box for a pow wow. They agreed that old Perky, the mule, could move the crate with an assist by three strong boys. As Blue Jack fetched Perky the mule, the other boys got ropes and an old pair of skis belonging to Little Jack, another Jack in town. Younger than the rest of the Jacks. Little Jack, then accompanied his friends back to the center of attention, with his skis. An essential contribution he thought even if he could not contribute much muscle to the enterprise. It was early evening so the boys were hurried by the fact that at nightfall accidents on the road were most common. Especially since the big crate sat firmly ensconced in the dirt and gravel. With youthful care, the skis were placed under the crate with much groaning and heaving with a spud bar, borrowed from Gray Jack's dad. Of course, Gray, Jack came along with the spud bar and was slightly chagrined that he was not summoned simultaneously as Red and Green Jack had been. Little Jack just smiled. Gray Jack was small too, but wiry and strong. The ropes were attached to the harnesses and tack the boys had assembled and placed on the strong body of Perky the mule. A great rope used to pull hay up and into the loft of Blue Jack's Dad's barn by pulleys was used to tie around the crate.

Then came the magnificent struggle. With shouts of encouragement and groans of exertion, the crate began to move along the dirt road. Perky pulled and tugged until the veins in her ears looked about to pop. Down the dirt road and up a little grade they went into Blue Jack's yard. The little troop with sweating brows maneuvered the box along the garden path until they came to the back of the barn. The boys exhaled great puffs of satisfaction and all rested on the blue crate, patiently waiting to be rejuvenated by nature's good graces.

Soon, the boys were exclaiming an unbridled desire to bust open the crate and have a look at its contents.

"No, we can't and won't. Just suppose someone comes by and they are looking for this blue box. In all truth, I would have to give it back to them unharmed and unopened. Let's just cover it with some hay and leave it here until all enquiries about it evaporate and fade away. It is probably just some books or crazy stuff from some poor oriental country."

The boys did as Blue Jack suggested. All the Jacks gave Perky a rub down and copious amounts of kudos for the old beast. Jumping around the barn to avoid old Percy's deposits they became the jumping jacks of Robsnest without even knowing it.

Most of the summer passed-by with no one asking around for the blue box. Even in school, the Jacks were tight lipped. Blue Jack's father did find the box and quizzed Blue jack mercilessly. After such an interval, his dad was won over to Blue Jack's side. The sheriff was way over in Riverton and no body in these parts took on the job of the constabulary. The whole affair became mute as winter rode in with a vengeance. Snow and ice covered everything, stopping everything, even the incessant inquiring of the other Jacks about the blue crate. Spring finally came with its wonderful aromas and greenery.

Coming around the barn one morning after collecting greens for his mom, Blue Jack noticed the blue box peeking through the moldering hay that covered it. No one had asked about it all winter. Surely it was his now. Finder's keeper's loser's weepers, kept rattling around his brain. He would ask his dad if they could now open the crate with the satisfaction, that no one wanted it.

In school, the other Jacks began to remember and talk about the blue crate. Blue Jack finally got permission from his dad to open the box. Blue Jack assembled all of his Jack friends, including Little Jack, at the back of the barn. When all of the colors had assembled, they began.

Just as they were about to open the box with a crow bar and maul, Blue Jacks father approached the crew with a grave look upon his face.

"Boys, there is a man out front that I think wants to talk to all of you."

With baited breath and pounding hearts, the little gaggle of Jacks went out front to confront the stranger. A giant of a man met them. His face was sun dried with a long beard, penetrating black beady eyes. He had a stub of a corncob pipe in his mouth and a brown stain on his lips from years of chewing tobacco. When he opened his mouth to speak his teeth were rotting and his tongue flailing dark, like the tail of a beaver. He shot out some spittle to those nearest him as he boomed out in a base drum voice.

"Boys, I am looking for a crate of ample proportions and great weight that I lost last year. I am certain it was some where in these parts. Your dad said you all may know of something of it's where abouts."

Blue Jack stepped forward and with quivering voice and trembling chin confessed they had found it and were saving it for the day the owner came by to collect it from them. Would a white lie tarnish my soul, he thought? All the boys looked sheepishly, as they quickly dropped the crowbar and spud bar along with the maul.

The old grizzly bear of a man continued.

"I ordered that item quite a while back from overseas, from the orient, cheaper than domestically. When it arrived in Riverton, I hired a freight wagon, and some teamsters to cart it up to my place in Whiskey Hollow. When it came up missing I made such a fuss that the freight company and teamsters all agreed to ante up enough cash to reimburse me for my loss. I then ordered the same item from New England and not internationally. It cost a might more, but I think I got a much better product. I use the item to alert my friends up in Whiskey Hollow of impending visits from the revenuers. I just came by on a hunch to tell you that the item is yours to keep. I have no loss in the matter and only wondered what happened to it. That freight company will be more careful in the future. They, of course, are gone. Probably out of business. They put the wagon and teamsters on the barge and left to who knows where?"

When the bear had finished, with all of his tobacco sputtering, all of the Jacks invited him to the unveiling of the crate.

"No, No. It is yours to have and to hold now. I want no part of it, and I have got to get going now. I got to buy a lot of sugar down at Henshen's store."

With a salute, the old codger was gone in his empty wagon towards Mr. Henshen's store.

"O.K. Guys lets have a go at it." Little Jack, blurted out as he turned and ran back to the barn. The other boys picked up their tools and followed in a state of mild shock over their good fortune.

When the colors had reassembled at the crate, a plan emerged.

"Jack, you remove the rest of the hay for a better look and then put the crow bar under that top brace," said Blue Jacks' dad.

For a moment, Blue Jack's father had forgotten their names, for all of the boys tried to grab the crowbar at once. Only little Jack was removing hay.

"O.K. Blue Jack you found it, so have the first go at it with the crowbar." His dad finally got it straight. Soon all of the boys were taking part in the dismantling of the blue box until a great cast iron bell in all of its glory was revealed. In unison the troupe ejaculated." WOW!"

"What are we going to do with it, Dad?"

"I don't know but how you got it up here I can't imagine. I can't see us putting it up in the barn, too heavy. Perky has gone bad on her feet so she can't help. I guess we will have to just leave it here until we can find a good place for it to finally rest."

After each boy ran his fingers over the great bell, they all sighed with deep moans of unhappiness the group left with down cast faces and trudged back to their respective homes to mull over their disappointment. They couldn't even ring it because it was resting on the ground.

The boys soon forgot about the bell as summer swims, picnics and girls invaded their lives. The bell only had visitors when one of the Jacks wanted to impress some nice young girl with their catch. It was better than bugs and muscle flexing to get an 'oh' or 'ah' from their special new found feminine associations.

Of course, the years passed, and the bell's influence diminished to only a dreamy historic remembrance. Little Jack grew up to be a football player of some note, Green Jack bought a greenhouse in Riverton after college. Red Jack joined the army and reached a high officer's rank. Gray Jack left town without finishing high school. Blue Jack finished college and seminary, then returned to Robsnest where he started a church of the full gospel persuasion. The congregation was small but mighty in the Lord. They built a church on land given to Blue Jack by his father. The bell was uncovered, cleaned, and polished.

Then with the aid of all able-bodied members, the bell was raised to the steeple and placed there with a mighty yoke to be rung on the first day of services. When that day arrived and all were in attendance the bell was rung vigorously but on the seventh clap the bell split up one side with a crack as thin as a piece of paper, damaging forever its melodic voice.

Afterwards, the bell was rung only on special days with only a cling, or clang, or even a clung, for nostalgia, but sounded to Blue Jack (Now called pastor Jack) as though it was saying," Sin no more." A reminder of the deception of hiding the bell he had perpetrated years before with the blue box. "The Bible says to learn to do good and sin no more." That was what this Jack was doing now.

BUDD THE GRASSHOPPER

B UDD THE GRASSHOPPER LIVED IN a great field full of high grasses and weeds. With very powerful legs and beautiful wings that enabled him to hop and fly all about the great field. Certainly, he epitomized the most impressive and lovely creature in all creation.

His only doubts came whenever Delovely the radiant and attractive social butterfly would flit out over the field bouncing in the air from flower to flower. Budd became jealous whenever Delovely, the beautiful social butterfly would come onto the scene. Budd was determined to be the most attractive bug in his universe. He found some wax in the woods that the bees had left behind and with much vigor applied it to his legs. Budd buffed his fine legs until they gleamed like the sun. Budd also washed his colorful wings in some stump water to bring out all their natural beauty. Budd continued his brilliant bathing by bedecking his proboscis with locally gathered pollen.

He also buffed and polished his high domed head until it gleamed. When finished he was a sight to behold. Hopping, and then flying all around the great field, Budd noticed all his friends were impressed by his new appearance. Some of his hopping Buddies both in truth and in jest declared to one and all that to look at Budd was comparable to looking at the sun.

"Cover your eyes," one would declare. "Here comes the sun," said another. "Bring out some tanning lotion," exclaimed a third. It was an eye-popping spectacle. Budd would hop high in the air with his great shiny legs flashing in the sunlight when there he would open his wings with a magician's flare. He displayed his powdery wings by twisting in flight and simultaneously quivering his proboscis. (A nose in the air for a flagrant flare thought Budd.) All in the field had to admit they had never seen a more beautiful and attractive flying bug. They all began to applaud his super antics of a breathtaking display of grandeur.

The next second all the bugs in the field became frozen into silence by the appearance of the loveliest form in all bugdom. The beautiful and comely social butterfly fluttered nearby and paled all those looking at her. The lovely Miss Delovely, the social butterfly of all the land came on the scene. She flitted past the assembly and smiled as she gained some height on an agreeable breeze.

The smile cut Budd in two that day. He knew in his heart he was no match for the dazzling Miss Delovely, the entire land's social butterfly. Budd felt humbled but not decimated by the event before his eyes. He would have to gather all his wits and resources to be looked upon by his peers as the prettiest bug in the field. Budd began to formulate in his little mind some plans to outwit the lovely Miss Delovely, the social butterfly. Budd determined he was not a dud and would move the grassy field even to the mud to find bugs to help him become more beautiful than the lovely Miss Delovely.

Budd set off through the high weeds and grasses hopping and flying looking for any bug that could help his beauty. He searched and inquired all that day, but no bug or insect would give to Budd any of their own beauty. The bees and wasps told him that if they gave up any beauty that they could not fulfill their duty and destiny. The beetles and dragonflies told him that they couldn't help because they were already as beautiful as any creature in the fields and didn't think a contest was important. Budd returned to his field of high grasses and weeds dejected and down hearted. The process was painful for Budd because he had so many things just handed to him without any exertion. It was an eye opener for Budd to see others enjoy their beauty and did not want to trade or exchange their beauty for any reason. His heart was so low that he was thinking of going down to the great pond where all the birds gathered to feast on bugs and tempted them by jumping high and flaunting them with his antics. "Who cares," said Budd out loud to no one specifically.

"I care," came an unexpectant response from above. Budd looked up and saw the very lovely Miss Delovely in all her satisfying array of colors and countenance. Her wings were gauze-like and contained the colors of the rainbow. In the sunlight, they appeared as fire and ice together fluttering ever so gently. It was all Budd could do take it all in and left him breathless. Finally regaining his composure, Budd could finally speak to Delovely as she hovered in mid air.

"I'm so plain and unattractive, and I have no beauty to offer the field or my friends," said Budd with near tears in his eyes. Budd looked down as though it was painful to continue to gaze upon the lovely Miss Delovely.

"You are beautiful to the fields and to your Creator. We all look upon you as the finest grasshopper in the field. We each must learn to look inside ourselves for the beauty that is important and not what is on the outside. We each have a destiny that calls for us to be as we are and not what someone else looks like. If you are all that you can be with what you have been given by the Creator then that is beauty."

Delovely the lovely social butterfly turned as she began to flit away and conclude by saying, "Find a lady hopper and settle down, If she loves you she will tell you each day how beautiful you are and that she has eyes for no one else, despite their coloring or form."

Delovely left the beautiful Budd with his mouth agape but with a changed heart. The social butterfly was last seen going from flower to flower bringing joy, sunshine, and beauty wherever she went.

MAGGIE'S PREDICAMENT

MARGARET (MAGGIE) MERRIMAN WAS A small girl from a small family, in a small town in a small state. She has a dad and mom and a sister and brother. She is average and yet unique.

Her granddad called her Peppy, and teased her occasionally as all granddads do. At seven or eight, Maggie actually enjoyed his teasing. However, a day came when every thing began to change.

It was about on her thirteenth birthday that Maggie began to notice things. Things began to change all around her. Her body, her mind, her friends, everything was changing. She didn't like to be teased anymore by anyone. Her hair, a deep, dark coppery red, was now unruly and she wanted it to grow long, even though her mother had always kept it short for convenience sake.

Daily reviews in her mirror only brought Maggie lower and lower in her self-esteem. She was certain it was an ugly face with her nose too short, her ears too big, and her teeth slightly protruding. This was the least of her ugly features. Maggie was very aware of her predicament, as some boys at school had made fun of her. At that juncture, she vowed she would never associate with boys for the rest of her life.

Maggie's mother told her to ignore all the taunts from boys and to formulate good thoughts about herself. This was much harder to do than to agree to. The nickname hurt her most. Her friends tried to convince her that it only meant they noticed her, and the name would eventually go away. Maggie knew how nicknames stuck and ultimately defined an individual that often stayed for life.

Maggie began her own program to avoid these taunts and jabs. It was a program of creams and ointments. Trying to rid herself of her predicament was not easy. She even tried mild acids and implements to cut away the ugliness. It left her with some minute scars as well as creating more attention to her face. Maggie spent the next few years looking in magazines and medical journals trying to find a cure for her ugly face.

Ice cubes were applied as well as a host of internal and external nostrums. Nothing worked so that Maggie kept her face turned down when approaching a group or she held up a magazine or paper when sitting. It all began to wear on the young lady as the years ticked by to the extent those social contacts became infrequent. Her parents tried to console her but were unable to penetrate her notion that she was ugly and repulsive. Even Granddad called her Lovey as his new nickname for her. Nothing worked.

It was one day while reading her Bible that she began to shed new light on her dilemma. The verse was in First Peter 3:3. This gave her the courage to negate outside appearances. Her hair, nose, ears, and forehead were not the things that portrayed her. Beauty was deeper than those things.

"Your beauty should not come from outside adornment such as braided hair and the wearing of gold jewelry and fine clothes. Instead it should be that of your inner self, the unfading beauty of a gentle and quiet spirit which is of great worth in God's sight."

These words of the Bible bore into the very inner being of Maggie and wiped away a myriad of misconceptions in a very short period. Maggie began to forget all about her facial disfigurement.

As the days and weeks flew by, Maggie became more and more gregarious. Maggie began to walk straight and proud, even going on a few dates with fellows. One fellow in particular was a target for the new and improved Maggie. His name was Henry or Hank as his friends called him.

Hank was of a medium build with an infectious smile that radiated white teeth. His hair was dark and slightly curly that accentuated a high, intelligent forehead. He had no chance once Maggie set her sights on the young man.

After an appropriate time of dating and then courting, Hank finally popped the question of matrimony. He pursued her until she caught him.

During the engagement period, they each began to open up to the other in the most meaningful ways. Discussions about children, finances, morals, and many other very pertinent topics. One night while on a date to a dance Maggie asked Hank what he saw in her. Hank was taken back by the question as he had told her many times how much he loved her.

"What I see is a person I will love all my life."

"That's not what I mean," Maggie replied. "What I want you to tell me is what do you see when you look at my face, and me" Maggie added quite seriously.

Hank took some time to answer this most interesting and probing question.

"I see a lovely face with character and beauty, also with virtue that accentuates those gorgeous eyes. Your smile is ravishing as well as infectious." With a deep sigh, he was sure he had adequately described his beloved and was shocked when she replied.

"No, No not all that stuff. What I want to know is what do you think about all my freckles plastered all over my face."

"Well to tell you the truth, I never really noticed that they were all over your face and I never thought they were a primary part of you. I always saw you through your eyes and never majored too much on any other facial features."

"Very good and thank you, Hank. That is what I have waited a lifetime to hear, and I am so glad it came from someone I will love all my life. No more Freckle Face from anyone."

Therefore, they lived happily every after, freckles and all.

The End

AN OAK TREE KISS

U SUALLY A SOUND FIRST WINDS its way through the maze of darkness and inactivity. This was determined to be a sound, by my fuzzy mind, as a bird's song or mating call. In an instant, I remembered who and where I was and that I had opened wide the window the night before to catch the balmy late evening breeze of spring. Before opening my eyes I tried to discern the other sounds that wafted through the window and settled on my sleepy thinking process. There was the sound of a far away truck walking through its gears. That next sound was the wind gently moving into and out of the branches and leaves of that old great oak in our front yard. What a sweetheart that old gal had been throughout my life here at home. Now she was making music to me as I was waking up on this precious spring morning. I thought of the many baskets of leaves I had raked up each fall under her outstretched limbs, but in the same instant the picture came to mind of me jumping high and landing safely and softly in the midst her life castings of leaves. I could kiss her for her sturdiness in holding by just one arm the ropes for my swing that once graced the shade underneath that part of our yard.

I opened one eye and saw the room was already flooded with that special warm blue spring light that only comes in June. I remembered that this day my family had all left very early to visit relatives several counties away and would be gone all day. They left me to tend the house and fulfill my paper route obligations this afternoon. WOW! I am free! My other eye popped open in the same movement that I reared up and out of bed, wild with excitement. My eye pained a little as it adjusted to the exquisite June morning's aura.

My mind was flooded with all the things I could do today. After all, I would be unencumbered with the presence and conservativeness of parents and siblings.

I quickly washed, dressed, and prepared for a most personal and singularly unique day. While wolfing down breakfast, my mind raced through a host of events that would satisfy my youthful longing for spontaneity and notoriety. Surely, the first order of the day would be to go out and give that big old oak tree a great big kiss. The old screen door squeaked opened and slammed shut as I took a huge deep breath of that exhilarating fresh morning air. I was ready now to give that mammoth mother of trees a bountiful buss on her beautiful blackened bark beneath her benefiting boughs. I walked towards her and then began to rethink my position.

Maybe later today I decided. I had always wanted to do something under these conditions, and it wasn't kissing the big oak. She would wait. She always had. I turned sharply around and headed back into the house trying to remember all of the things I would need. Upstairs to the bathroom I went and quickly found the beach towel folded neatly and placed underneath of all the others as though it might have been hidden. I then proceeded hurriedly into my room and to that lower dresser drawer. Where oh where did I put it last year? Ah, at last the blue swim suit in the back of the drawer. These were great trunks with a wide waistband and shiny material all around except the two stripes. One on each side. White. Just right. The goggles were to be found in the basement, and an umbrella was waiting in the hallway. All of these items I tucked under my arm as the whole scenario began to gel in my thoughts. Out the door again and around towards the garage I moved impulsively. In the garage, I reached up and got Dad's telescoping ladder, used for the big jobs. It was aluminum, and not as heavy as I remembered it when doing household chores. I carried it outside to the side of the garage and climbed up to survey all the territory and its peculiarities. When the whole plan was secure in my mind, I returned to the garage and closed the door. I began to undress and dress as fast as I thought was appropriate. I tied the towel around my neck. It immediately became a cape with that magical, supernatural ability needed by crusaders. I fastened it with a big safety pin to keep it secure. The trunks were a good fit and the goggles felt great. I grabbed the umbrella, raced back to the ladder, and up I shot like a streak of lightning. Capt. Marvel and Batman couldn't have done better. As I neared the edge of the roof, I looked over and was glad for the umbrella just in case. I needed to back up to the top of the garage roof and thereby have a downward run to pick up speed. I was ready. The Superman of Adam's Road had covered all the bases; thought out all the consequences; and mused over every detail. Now all that was left was the flight and the glory.

Down the roof, I dashed at full speed. The beach towel cape was fluttering in the wind. My head was lowered and of course very determined. The umbrella was up and I could feel its resistance over my head as it filled with air. The sky was filled with those clouds that are washing the day, white and fluffy. They seemed to be everywhere. I gave a giant leap into the waiting arms of the warm spring atmosphere at the roof's edge. I could feel both the pull of gravity, and the upward tugging of the umbrella. The outstretched cape and kicking feet were not propelling any part of this exhibition, to my dismay. Suddenly the ground began to rocket towards me as doom and despair closed in upon me. Swoosh and pop went my overhead friend, no doubt collapsing, without warning, at the same instant, the umbrella began to pull up, as though God were drawing me closer to Him. This sudden change of events slowed everything down to slow motion in comparison with the microsecond before. I landed with a medium thud, only to have some of the wind knocked out of me. No broken bones or lacerations, I decided after a few seconds of examination and reorientation. What happened?

What kept me from breaking every bone in my body? Why does my pride hurt and not my whole body?

Catching my breath, I finally found out that no one had witnessed this little drama. I looked to see what had saved the day and me. The umbrella had collapsed, and simultaneously a far-reaching limb from the old oak tree had caught it in her grasp. She slowed down my descent just enough to break what could have been a nasty fall. I was glad. I was happy. I was grateful. I was fulfilled. Breathing excitedly, I jumped up and ran over to that old tree. Without thinking, I put my arms full around as much of the old tree as I could reach. With face on the tree and lips on her bark, I proceeded to give a great big thank you kiss. Well, it's over. I tried and missed the mark, but no one needed to know. I looked up. There, next door was Mrs. Shipley, with mouth agape. She had seen all and would report all, to the powers that be. Mother and father would find a way to punish me for being so brazen with foolish overtones. Oh well. It was one fine spring morning I would never forget, and that has to be worth something.

KING OF THE SQUARES
(LORD OF THE RINGS??)

IGHTING SEEMS TO BE THE norm for boys. We see at
an early age, the possession of toys is not negotiated;
they are fought over. Later the same type of struggle takes
place in games or sports. Grabbing, hitting, running all are
part of the game to dominate an opponent. Most of the
games have some kind of rules of engagement, but in real
life the rules are omitted. In real life, deception, hurt, and
nefarious advantages become the norm. This is the basis for
this story about the struggle of squares.

Alvin was smart, and clever with words. Alvin was big
for his age but very clumsy. Alvin tried to be likable but
failed at every turn. His parents were both employed in
academia. They were teachers in subjects like mathematical
probabilities and psychology; locally labeled eggheads. Alvin
was tainted by his parent's reputation. Alvin was a square.

Richie was a friend of Alvin's. Richie was small for his
age and thin for his height. Richie was the last to be chosen
when a team was formed unless Alvin was present. Then he
was next to the last. Richie was what one would call poor.
He had patches on his pants, and his shoes were resoled
frequently. His shirts were made by his grandma out of
discarded feed sacks. Richie was quick but lacked strength.
Richie was a square.

There were a number of squares at school in the little
town of Cumberville. It was thought that years ago the
town had carried a great burden of somesort; therefore, the
name of Cumberville. Now the town was associated with the
surrounding cucumber fields. What ever the origin of the
town's name it apparently was now forgotten. A great burden

would adequately describe the plight of the squares since most of the folks in the area were infatuated by sports. If you played sports you were held in high esteem. If you didn't play in any sport, you were a square to town and student alike.

In school there was a circle of bullies that took great pleasure in harassing the boys labeled squares. The chief agitator was Ray Bullerton. Ray was big for his age and husky. He failed a grade so that made him a year older than his classmates. Ray excelled at sports and was the school's darling because of it. Ray's muscular attributes and sport acumen where not enough acclamation for him. Ray with his flashing teeth that impressed the girls to fatuous glee found his self worth elevated even more when harassing the squares. Ray's round puffy face would break out with grins and guffaws when knocking books out of the arms of Richie and his group. Ray and some of his circle would find their greatest intimidation in confiscating some of the square's bikes and raising them up the school's flagpole. This brought belly laughs from the offending circle of toughs and near tears to the little band of squares. The powers that be, looked upon the pranks with jaundiced eye but were handicapped by the town's love of sports. Bullies seemed to reign as Lords. The schools apparent endorsement of the toughs actually reinforced the circle of ne'er-do-wells to commit more acts of cowardice upon the small band of squares.

During the summer when the squares hoped for a respite, the acts of fulmination from the bullies continued. Bikes were found in ditches, great sport was directed to squares at the swimming pool, making fun of individual bodies, library books scattered at the library and on and on.

Ray found that to hide around the school when some of the squares were hoping to play some scrub baseball was a special treat. He would pick out one of the squares and provoke a fight. Most of the smaller boys would scatter home when the selected square was put through the ordeal. The conflict would finally cease when the square would yell

UNCLE and concede defeat with a promise to Ray not to come to the playground for a determined time. The small or square boys were glad when Ray only determined a time of a month or two. It was painful and humiliating, but one had to live in the real world and try to make peace even with the most brutal of adversaries. That remained true until one day in the fall at Cumberville.

The squares agreed to meet secretly in a place outside town.

"We have got to find a way to outsmart those bullies and jocks so we can live in peace," said Peter, one of the smaller square boys.

He continued." We are all getting to be ostracize by the other students who are beginning to take up where the bullies are leaving off. It is a contagious sort of thing. I have tried everything to avoid Ray and his circle of ruffians. I have even fought Ray, the ring leader, in the hopes that when I cried out 'uncle' he would quit picking on me." But, to no avail. "I just don't want to suffer another year."

Peter was small with carrot red hair, and freckles in great abundance. This combination seemed to ignite detrimental teasing to the point of tears for Peter. Peter's freckled face was pointed out by the bullies as the result of Peter's wetting the bed or some other nefarious activity. All lies, of course.

Richie was listening carefully and trying to formulate a plan of action to negate Ray and his circle of toughs. Before he could add to the discussion, Alvin gave his opinions.

"I tried to get my dad to buy a big ferocious dog to protect me but after much thought it became apparent to me and with my dad's insight that a dog for that purpose would have only minimal times to be effective. His advice was to bulk up to be as tough as the bullies and get to the point of whipping them. The thought of me doing that made me nauseous." "Maybe one of you guys could do that for the benefit of all of us."

There was some mumbling and murmuring of the dissenting kind.

"None of us are that big or strong, even I couldn't get that strong before we all get in school," said Alvin with a squeak in his voice.

Finally Richie chimed in.

"I think we must defeat our foes with the advantage that we have been empowered with; our brains."

There was a time of complete silence as the words sank in and began to take hold. Each square began to think of his own intelligence and pondered about the talents each possessed, such as the good grades they were getting in school. For a long time no one offered any more comments for fear of disclosing any short comings in their own mental prowess. When the silence became deafening, Peter spoke up.

"I would like to nominate Richie as King of the squares, to out-wit and out maneuver Master Ray and his circle of punks."

A cry of agreement went up from the little assembly of afflicted boys, including bucktoothed Chuckie. Chuckie was a boy, tall for his age and with a set of choppers that any beaver would envy. His large, owl-like glasses didn't help matters any. He also had a high forehead that proposed early baldness.

Richie didn't know quite how to react. It was certainly a sign of popularity but also responsibility, maybe too heavy to bear. This honor must be turned into a successful conclusion. His head began to fill with ideas as the realization of the brash turn of events became jelled in his mind.

"Why don't you ask your brother to stand up and fight for us?" Richie said as he looked at Peter with great expectations.

Peter was ready with an answer almost before Richie had finished.

"I already tried that, and my brother told me to fight my own battles."

Alvin was ready with another answer.

"Let's always go around in two and threes with a club or stick and if any of them try to beat up on us we will fight back and hurt them so bad they will stop giving us a hard time."

Chuckie thought a sneak attack on one of the ring of brutes would hurt him so bad they would be afraid to try something on any of us.

The discussions continued for a long time until Richie summed up the discussion with a very insightful comment.

"Boys, don't you see that all our comments about our common dilemma resolve around fight and might. We are not the kind that should return bullying with violence. We must find our strong points and use that to overcome this hardship. What do we possess that they don't? When we discover that we will use it to overcome this adversary."

There was mumbling and murmuring that reflected their negative and defeatist position.

"I'm tired," said Chuckie.

The other boys also seemed to be defeated too until Richie piped up with, "I think I have a good idea but would like to sleep on it and allow the plan to come together so I can explain it to all of you tomorrow, after we have had a good night's sleep."

With that plan in mind the boys separated feeling much better about their future. They all agreed that it was a good idea to have Richie as King of the squares. To send one of their own into the ring with an attaboy was the groups mental vision. Shades of David and Goliath.

Richie returned home with a peeled eye at every turn in the road. Reaching his little house at the edge of town he sought out his mother. When he found her in the kitchen, he wondered if he should pore out his heart at the point of his mom making supper. She listened intently with that all knowing face and blue piercing eyes.

Richie's mom was not old, but he thought of her as quite ancient. She must have lived many years to be so wise and correct, thought the young boy. She too was small of stature with graying hair. Mom was always busy doing things that no one else would do or so mundane no one wanted to do. She never took or asked for any credit for all the good meals served, or clothes washed or tidying up after everyone continually. She just did it all, knowing her rewards came in little golden ways others might not see. Her most precious activity was reading her Bible every night with a cup of hot tea by her elbow when the house had settled down and the chores were finished. That was when her face shone with youth and beauty like no other time. The family knew not to interrupt her then for she was 'gassing up', as she called it.

Richie knew that in the kitchen his mom was all his. Here, she was queen of the world, knowing all and seeing all. She acknowledged his presence with a smile accompanied by a majestic nod of her head. Wiping her hands on a towel, she spoke.

"Richie you look perplexed. Is there anything I can do?"

The boy knew that his mom had already guessed he was in a difficult predicament. His mom was like that!

"Mom, I do have a problem."

Mom sat down and told him to tell her all about it. (supper could wait.)

At this juncture, Richie poured out his heart. With mom listening intently, Richie felt the burden lighten because she was interested in his problem. When the boy had finished his narrative, mom reached out and drew the lad into her arms with a hug of bearish proportions.

"Of coarse I have some suggestions but first we must pray about this situation. We will pray that the ring leader as well as the other bullies are blessed with joy and peace with love abounding. The Bible tells us to pray for those that we perceive as those that despitfully abuse us." And so they did, then and there in the kitchen.

"Tonight before you go to bed I expect you to ask for more guidance from above that will give you boys a clearer path to follow. No one ever regretted doing things the Lord's way."

And so it was. Richie was onto a plan.

The next day the boys all met by prearrangement on their bikes out in the country. A place away from bully eyes.

School would be starting in only days, and the boys wanted to enjoy some free time away from danger, before school started. They put down their bikes and gathered on a grassy, sunny hillock to discuss Richie's plan for freedom from the bully ring.

When Richie explained it in detail he was met by a wall of silence.

He had shown them that nothing would change unless they did.

"If we do nothing, everything will stay the same." They agreed.

"If we meet violence with violence we only begat more violence. We all are very clever and smart and go to church. It must be from these strengths that we have to overcome our nemeses. My advice is that we continue to lift up these boys in prayer. When school starts, we will determine if any of them need tutoring to stay eligible for sports. We will offer to become team managers and helpers in anyway possible to be an asset to the teams. We can ask the coaches if we can help make the teams to excel both physically and mentally. We could help with the cheer leading or scope out the opposing teams. We must become a monolith of service and helps."

The little group sat in the late summer sunshine agonizing in their minds all the thoughts and visions presented to them by their friend and leader. Could the King of the squares defeat the Lord of the ring? It would have to be answered sooner or later.

The boys left the sunny hill to return to homes in warmer shades of uncertainty. With much encouragement from Richie the squares implemented the plan. Each boy sought out one of the offending bullies to the surprise of all the school. The squares were first rebuffed. But, when the square boys explained their actions, they were still met with doubt and skepticism.

The squares prayed each morning and met each evening for progress reports. It was slow going.

Richie had selected Ray as his target of love and service. The two boys fit together like oil and water. Richie had acquired a nice set of bruises and even a black eye. One afternoon as Richie was trying out for track, he noticed the fastest runner, Ray, sitting on the side lines. When Richie approached the bigger boy, Ray's scowl became even grimmer. With a certain hesitancy, Richie spoke first.

"Why aren't you on the track, practicing for the school's big meet this month? You are the fastest boy in school."

Ray answered with a voice Richie had never heard before. It was filled with painful emotion.

"I'm not going. No use practicing. I just found out my family has to move in the near future. My dad lost his job again, and we have to move up-state where his new job is located."

Richie saw a sort of halo surround the two boys sitting together. As tough as it might be for Ray, it looked to Richie like answered prayer. No fighting, no scheming, no deceptions, only a resolution to an unsolvable situation.

When Ray left Cumberville, his bully friends all seemed to merge into the rest of the young people of the town. None of those boys took up where Ray left off. Most of them showed signs of cowardice from time to time. Without a leader they became impotent. A ring without a ring leader became a broken circle devoid of power.

The band of squares all grew up healthy and wise. Prayer counts even for the small things of this life. Alvin became a very renown Doctor of medicine specializing in the health of athletes. Chuckie became a very prominent Law Officer in

Cumberville and later as a State Trooper. Peter grew up and bulked out to become a national hero in football. He became a tight end nicknamed, the 'flying flame'. Richie grew up to became a minister of the Gospel. Pastoring a large church he used the example of the King of the Squares versus the Lord of the Ring, as a successful teaching tool. Persistence and prayer really work.

The End

DANDY

I T WAS A MISTAKE OF disastrous proportions that would affect me forever, thought the boy. Hot tears tried to spring up of the eleven-year old, sixth grader, as he stood behind the fence. He had almost learned how to control this particular emotion and was successful this time by taking his shirtsleeve and wiping it across his face as an emotional dust rag. The face was an important weapon thought the young man as he pursed the mouth and wrinkled his face into a scowling mask of pugilistic fury. He carefully looked around the fence to see whether way home was clear.

Even though it was early autumn, the air was crisp in his new town. He had to play this scene many times before and was growing tired of the threats and ridicule. He had just started school a few days before and that's when this trouble began. In his class every one had to write their name, address and other relevant information the school needed on a yellow form. When they were finished, several of the class members collected the papers and deposited them with the teacher. The boy's collector was Ray, the class bully. He was snickering under his breath as he completed his task. Sneers fitted Ray's face as his nose and mouth melted together easily with the accompanying nasal sounds of a snake. "What's the problem." Said the teacher as Ray pointed to the top document that was the new boy's. She scanned the paper and then looked up and gazed directly at the newest class member and said, "You must write your full given name and not your nickname because this will be entered your official record."

"That is my real, given, full name, mam," came back the reply.

"How pleasant. Can you tell us how you came to be named DANDY?"

Then, came a few laughs and snickers.

"Yes mam. My Dad saw me for the first time at the hospital when I was born and said, what a dandy! The name stuck."

The room was now filled with laughter and loud guffaws to the point where teacher had to restore order.

The last few days were filled with embarrassment and terror. The room bully threatened to beat Dandy up after school today and was now seen coming to the fence where a quick look caused a discovery. Dandy came out, met the big-faced twit and waited for the fight to escalate. It did. Bully pushed the smaller boy. Badly out classed by weight and age, Dandy was struggling to get up when a shriek and tiger-like fury attached itself to the aggressor. Lighting fast arms and nails were everywhere on the bully bringing pain and discomfort. His small brain quickly determined that someone must need him somewhere else and he got up and out to his own voice, declaring, "ouch and wow!"

Dandy looked at the author of this turnaround event and it was a girl from his room.

Dandy emitted a *"thanks"* and an offer to carry her books the rest of the way to her home. She accepted.

"What's your name," as they began the trek homeward.

With a smile that warmed him throughout she said, "My father loved me too. When I was born, He named me Sweetie."

Dandy could feel the healing happening all over his being.

The End

THE DARK AND THE DEEP

I FELT TIRED AND EXHAUSTED. No excuse would deter my wife in her pursuit of fulfilling this vision. She finally informed me that she would do it by herself if I wouldn't participate. Well, this put me over the edge and forced me to get involved in this adventure, like it or not. Therefore, I found myself each Thursday evening after a long day's work, heading over to the dive shop that we had contracted to teach and certify us as scuba divers. The deal was that once each week, for six weeks, we would gather after work and set our minds and bodies to the task of absorbing all the information and schooling required to become certified. This time was spent in viewing videotapes; going over material we had read the week before and then taking a test on all that information. After a few hours engaged in these kinds of academic activities, we adjourned to a large indoor pool where the real aquatic exercises took place. Into the pool, we jumped, where we completed many laps of swimming with visions of underwater adventures in far-off places dancing in our heads. We finished these cerebral and physical assignments for a period equal to six training days. After reading the designated book and passing, all the quizzes we were finally ready for the five required open water dives. Our SSI certification mandated these dives to receive our final approval as sport scuba divers. My wife, daughter, and I spent one entire, hot, August, Sunday at a rock quarry, executing these dives under the watchful eyes of our instructors. Somehow, through the sweltering day and murky, muddy waters of the quarry we all passed.

We soon began to talk of all the places we would now go to expand our skills and enjoy the fruits of our labors.

Discussions about the Midwest as possible destinations wore on as did the months. It was eventually decided that warm semi-tropical locales would be more desirable. The Cancun-Cozumel area was finally selected because of a variety of reasons and for several years we enjoyed that area, one week each, at vacation time. Great dives. Good weather. Fine food. Eventually, we concluded that it would be prudent to widen our diving horizons and try to experience other scuba Meccas.

Grand Cayman seemed like the next logical place. A packaged trip was available. Great dives like the North Wall. Unique Sting Ray city. Sunken ships. Shore dives. Night dives. Grottoes to explore. Turtle farm and museums to see. Off we went in the fall of 1992.

We arrived by plane in Georgetown. A short ride to our hotel and then the settling in process. Soon, we were renting a car from a rental place across the road from the hotel. We continued to develop our sightseeing and shore diving skills. This gave us an opportunity to become accustomed to our diving gear as well as the various dive shops around the island. We also had to discipline ourselves to drive on the left side of the road, as the British originally settled the island. All this activity finally gave us the incentive and courage to sign up for a night dive. I welcomed this adventure because the days had been so hot and uncomfortable. This was also our chance to experience something new and exciting in the world of scuba.

Phyllis and I waited until evening and then met at the appointed place of departure. At the dock, we all loaded our equipment on the boat and set out into the fading evening. The heat of the day went down, as did the sunlight. We all busily attended to and set up the various pieces of diving equipment. The B.C. vest and tank all had to be checked and secured in the prescribed manner. The weights had to be calculated and attached to our belts. Flippers, snorkels, flashlight and masks at our sides for their soon to be utilized assigned tasks. Movement and activity on the boat just before a dive is hectic. Everything must be perfect. Subsequently, the dive master called us to order for his instructions and directions. We are now all ears.

"This dive will be in about 35 feet of water. You will drop straight down because of the absence of currents at this destination," he went on. "At the bottom will be a circular coral reef that looks like a miniature volcano. Use your flashlights to go slowly around this jutting coral. This will take about 3o minutes. Do not use your flashlight close to the waters surface because of attracting unwanted predators and jellyfish. These creatures you want to avoid. I will have a Strobe light under the boat for your benefit to facilitate your ascent later. Now lets all get into the water, go down, and enjoy."

That was music to my ears. I tied on a little chemical light to the top of my B.C. vest. I had also purchased one for Phyllis. The one that Phyllis had did not work when we broke the capsule. Therefore, she had no chemical light on her B.C. vest as I did. Well, I would stay close by her to protect her and keep her from slowing down the expedition. We needed to hurry because the people were going off the boats aft platform like rapidly exiting frogs at my pond. Splash. Splash. Each diver went as they entered the water with the open scissors-like leap into the inky black sea water. "We are always last," I thought, as I inched my way towards the jump off point. I would need some extra time anyhow to descend, because of the great difficulty I had clearing my ears as the depth increased. Finally, I jumped in with one hand over my mask and the other hand on the B.C. vest controls.

The water was warmer than it seemed only minutes ago as I watched others submerge into the dark briny liquid. Now, under the water I could see other divers chemical lights below me. The winking of the boat's strobe light, placed strategically beneath the hull was easily noticed. It was functioning as a homing beacon, just as the dive master had said.

After descending a few feet, I began to encounter my usual difficulties of descent.

My ears began to hurt immediately because of the rapid descent. I therefore had to slow my descent by adding air to my B.C. vest. Remembering the dive masters caution, I deduced I was still too close to the surface to use my flashlight to read the time. The light on board was not enough to permit my watch's dial to glow. The console we use for depth and air pressure was not bright enough to read. My ears stopped hurting; therefore, I let some air escape from the vest to recommence a slow descent. I tried to swallow and hold my nose with gentle air pushes to clear the ears that were hurting almost continuously. Someone had said that if I stretched my neck from side to side that it would help clear the ears. My hurting ears took all of my attention with all kinds of gyrations to equalize the pressure in my ears. No success.

It suddenly occurred to me that I could no longer see the strobe light from the boat. I thought that I must have turned around or that maybe I was too deep now to see it. I finally turned on the little flashlight to check my time and saw that about eight minutes had elapsed. I now had about two minutes to get to the bottom and find my partner, Phyllis. Surely, they would all be just under me, only a few more feet down. I turned off the little light and continued to struggle with clearing my ears by going through more facial grimaces. My whole being was focused on reaching the bottom and regrouping with the other divers. Just a few more feet and only another minute more, I thought, as I fought the constant on again and off again pain in my ears. I again turned on the flashlight to shine down into the depths to see whether the bottom was in sight. The beam appeared as a stick of light in the darkness, ending a few feet away. It illuminated nothing. It now was imperative that I gather as much information as possible so that I could make a rational decision. My light was now on my console and I could read the dials. The pressure was good. I still had 1700 pounds of air. The other dial was not too good. My feet touched the bottom as I read the depth gauge at 65 feet. I tapped it with my finger to see whether the reading was correct. No change. I stretched out in a horizontal position and thrusted the lit flashlight in front of me. I saw a coral reef moving; at least I thought it was moving. Upon scrutiny, I determined it was I that was moving at a rather rapid pace. I was 65 feet down, in a current, drifting. I was detached from the rest of the group, and I had not surfaced after being separated from my missing partner for the required number of minutes. I was alone and lost.

It comes over you like a cold wet cloth. The reality that I had done something wrong and now was in trouble because of it. It also was clear that others would be adversely affected very soon if I didn't make some quick and precise actions immediately. To save face was dominant in my thinking. Do everything by the book, now, I thought. I began my ascent to the surface, slowly. I watched the bubbles rise from my regulator. That was the speed that I allowed the black sea to bring me to the surface. I used the flashlight sparingly because of the earlier admonition that it would attract unwanted ocean creatures. At fifteen feet, I stopped to decompress for a few minutes and to take one last look at all of my gauges. Plenty of air and about 20 minutes into the dive. It wouldn't be so bad when I popped to the surface and swam over to the boat with one of my long and clever explanations of what had happened to me. I thought of the joyous reunion that was soon to take place as I traveled up those last fifteen feet to the surface.

Bobbing to the surface I prepared myself to look in all directions for the waiting boat. I could feel the surface swell and ebb as the sea began its lifelike movements against my body. Looking through my facemask, I could not see anything. Even the sheeting effect of water that occurred there when I surfaced could not be detected in the blackness that I found myself. I kicked my swim fins in such a way that turned me about in 360 degrees. No lights on the surface and only the faintest suspicion of some stars in the sky to assure me that I was truly on the surface of a great pulsating sea at night. The swells would bring me high on the crest of water where I would strain to look intently in a new direction each time. Then I would be let down in a trough of water where my thoughts would rush in to give me various mental pictures of my dilemma or demise. After some time I spotted far in the distance some lights that appeared to be in a step formation. They began low, went up a step, then another, and then proceeded down in the same fashion. It was the outside lighting riggings of the boat that I so desperately needed. I began to swim with all my might in that direction to counter the current that seemed to be taking me farther away. I swam and swam until my lungs heaved and burned. I felt that little progress was being made and at this rate, I would never make it. I looked longingly at those lights as I rested for a moment. My facemask cleared up as I strained to peer at the far away hope. It suddenly dawned on me that I was looking not at a boat, but at the outside lights of a far away hotel on land. Too far to swim and be saved. I turned around and began to swim hard in the opposite direction to renew my search for my lost boat. From time to time, I would stop and hold up the flashlight as high as possible when on a sea crest and turn it on as I waved it back and forth. To no avail. I swam harder and more diligently than before, knowing that with each stroke I might crest high on a wave and see my goal. I again became exhausted to the point of feeling nauseated. I rested and began to think of all the awful things that might happen to a person lost out here on the high sea.

I didn't have a dive suit on, only a thin stretchy suit of cloth; therefore, I was exposed to the feel of the arms of the dark fluid all around and under me. I imagined the jaws of some shark coming close to my vulnerable, exposed legs and evaluating them for its midnight snack. I was sure I could feel it pass close to me. It didn't come straight in because of all the jellyfish that had been attracted by my flashlight swimming just a few inches away. The sky seemed even darker than earlier. Could that be a harbinger of a storm brewing up just over the unseen horizon? I had lost track of time as I braved the elements again by turning on the minuscule light. As I waved it frantically in the great unobserved void about me, a thought came over me like a wave. I was swimming away from shore and farther from the only place, I was sure that I could be saved. I turned rapidly once again towards shore and anxiously peered through my facemask for the lights of some far away safe hotel. As I strained to see those tiny pinpoints of hope, I noticed a large round searchlight shining to my left. With a quick kick of my flippers, I was looking straight at a silver ribbon of hope. An all-seeing eye in the night. I immediately lifted my little electric torch, waved it for the few prescribed seconds, and then turned it off to avoid the stinging, biting creatures laying in wait for scuba novices. It kept shining like a puncture in the darkness. I again repeated my light on, wave and now a vocal shout for help that was painful, both physically and emotionally. I held my breath to better hear the signal from the boat that they were on the way. As I strained to decipher that long awaited sound, the great sea eye went out and all was dark again.

I had noticed that my watch indicated I had been out of the boat only about an hour, but I was suspicious that the watch was keeping bad time. It seemed much longer. My next course of action was to gently swim in the direction of the recently disappeared probing beacon of illumination. It was difficult to swim, because all of my reserves had been consumed in the preceding spurts of desperation to get to a point of safety. I had also failed to pump up my BC vest to reserve air and the fear of rupturing the vest's bladder. I felt slightly confused now as I carefully swam in a manner that was slow and calculated. I wanted to be in a position of quiet so that I would hear any calls or sounds that might travel in my direction.

Each moment in that ebony fluid was like an hour. My mind wanted to race off in all directions of negative despair. Satan is the prince of coming attractions; all negative

My B.C. vest was feeling more cumbersome as I mulled over the options that were now available to a person lost at sea. My weight belt began to emit a sensation of hands about my waist pulling me down in the deep abyss. The air tank strapped on my back was my only comfort, as it would provide air if and when I was pulled beneath the billowing waves of an angry sea. My unprotected legs felt elongated to the point that they were invading the homes of the creatures of the deep.

At some point, I knew I had to pray, to prevent the natural mind from flooding the mind of hope. It wasn't that I was more important than anyone else. Or even more deserving. Everyone has the right to hope and to have faith in God. I began with some scriptures than pertained to His ability, yesterday, today, and forever. I ended with a reminder that this was the one He loved calling out. I rested for a moment. My throat was salty and dry from shouting to the Lord in the night ocean air. In my physical and mental exhausted state, I wasn't sure, but I thought I heard a voice that was carried on the wind. I heard my name in the thick darkness coming to me on the tops of surrounding waves in a pulsating effect. Dick, shine your light so I can see you. Keep it on so I can locate and swim to you." The voice shot out towards me. Someone else was in the water coming to me. He was swimming towards my held up flashlight. The helper on the dive boat grabbed my BC vest and me and preceded to super-inflate it to the point I bobbed up on top of the water. "I was afraid to put too much air in it and have it explode," I said in relieved, yet ignorant voice. "That's OK, He said." "Help is on the way."

My helper in the water was an experienced diver and swimmer. He said he swam over a mile every day to keep in shape. I was glad. Soon, a boat came to the spot that I had been found and taken aboard. This boat had shone a spotlight on me earlier, but thought I was a fisherman because the light kept going out. The boat had about eight divers, and they all seemed to look at me as the odd one out. Each appeared to be so young and yet so experienced. I was humiliated when it was revealed in causal conversation that no one had been lost like this for a long time. After about fifteen minutes, I was reunited with my original boat and patiently waiting, praying wife. All of my comrades, eventually, agreed it could have happened to anyone with the under current so strong. I was safe and wiser for the ordeal.

On the way back to shore, the talk weaved and bobbed towards the idea that the lucky, found seafarer was to buy the finders a case of beer. As those sentences drifted in my direction, my thoughts could not help but flash back to the tense time I had so recently weathered. I wanted to thank someone for the rescue and yet a case of beer was so temporary. No place to buy any out there anyway. I had thanked everyone profusely, and they all would soon go their own ways. My real help was from a divine source and thanks were only the beginning. Praise the Lord!

LIBERATING LEGS

I BELIEVE THAT EVERYONE GETS A chill or a jab from Mr. Death before that final trump calls them to the other side. As the years roll on and the experiences increase, one is prone to appreciate the celebration of living more emphatically. The first time that brush with mortality happens, all too often we take the event in stride without much comment or ceremony. Only later do we have the privilege to look back and weigh the event as a personal miracle that can teach us about the merciful hand of our Creator. I was only seven years old when that first time crept into my life without any warning.

My brother Billy was ten years old when I was seven. He was involved in several activities that I was too young to participate. The younger child looks to the older for projects and endeavors more difficult than the ones presented to his younger brother's age group. This results in messed up deals and his unwanted presence in the child caste system. This was evident when Billy and I would on Saturdays board a bus in our little town on the outskirts of Cincinnati and travel to the center of that metropolis. We disembarked from the bus at the end of Central Parkway and walked the block to the very active YMCA. This building was large and full of events and activities for young men of all ages. When we arrived, we were separated into age groups and sent off for a day filled with movement. I wondered what the older guys where doing and why I couldn't be with Billy. "Too rough and tumble", I was told. "Not old enough," was a favorite reply. "Too small," was the classic retort. We seven-year-old boys still had a lot of fun.

We played games, had gym classes, and art projects. One of my favorite exercises, besides eating lunch, was swimming classes. It was in the basement of that old downtown building. When in the swimming pool area you could look up at the ceiling and see several large areas of round glass bricks. These areas allowed the daylight to come into the pool area. A surprise came to me later when I found out that the glass translucent bricks where on the surface and a part of the sidewalk in front of the building. It was a mystery to me when I would look up and see people's shadows crossing those glass bricks that they didn't fall through to the water below. They never did

At seven, I had developed a certain modicum of modesty. Even Mother was not to see certain parts now. If a boy's fly was open, it produced such an embarrassment that flushed faces and lightening quick movements were the order of the moment. So demeaning was this event that the coded signal for its existence was developed. When "XYZ" was spoken in a low tone in your direction, immediate action was taken. This meant, examine your zipper. With red face and fumbling fingers, the targeted individual went through the motions to correct the degrading scenario. Only a few false alarms brought sanity back in the xyz warning. Modesty awakened and flowering seemed to be the best course when only seven.

The first time at the Y, we were given lockers and told of the things we were going to do. The hour before lunch was designated for me to be swim time. I thought that was good because of the appetite that comes with swimming. We assembled in the basement and shown our lockers.

We were told to undress and come into the pool, sans any clothes. This meant in the natural. The buff. Birthday suit. When they said you need not bring any swimsuits I must have thought they would be provided. With towel in hand, draped in front of me, I cautiously proceeded to the pool area. Others had the same idea as they looked behind them for any peekers or gawkers. The counselor told us the rules of the pool and paired us off with buddy partners. Soon all of us had to discard our towel-draped sanctuary and leap into the water. Because of my age, I had to stay in the shallow end and splashed about with abandonment. Most of the counselor's supportive attention was focused on the older and more advanced boys. They needed help in the various swimming techniques. We younger boys were satisfied to just play around the shallow end. I learned very little in this short period of time before going to camp, except that to try to keep covered by the towel was probably in vain.

Camp was for boys nine years old and up. I didn't qualify. Mother was sure if we petitioned the right people, at the right time that an exception would be made. My Dad was also confident that a likable boy like me would be able to go off to camp with his older brother for two weeks. He seemed to tackle the obstacle with energy and vigor. Calls were made and letters written. Only later in life when I had children did I realize why father was so persistent to send off his two sons for two weeks of camp. It was a vacation for someone, but whom?

Soon it was apparent that Dad had touched all the right buttons and signed the necessary papers allowing me to attend camp before my time. Soon the house was filled with activity to send the boys to YMCA camp in the hills of Kentucky far away. Nametags had to be sewn into all our clothing. Little kits were assembled for writing home, for personal hygiene, and for first aid emergencies. After many days, all was ready and packed for the trip to camp.

WE rolled into camp after an excited drive through the northern Kentucky countryside. Before me was the YMCA camp in all its glory. It was a sight to behold for a seven-year-old boy. The lawns were clean, mowed, and expansive. I could see tennis courts and ball fields. Basketball hoops and badminton nets didn't escape my eagle eye. The cabins were white and neatly in a row. In the center of the area was the meeting hall and dining room. Close by, on a little slope was a huge swimming pool complete with fence and grassy area. I could easily envision myself here, free as a bird. Two whole weeks of frolic and camaraderie with the BIG boys here I could fly.

Soon we were signed up and settled in. With only a few verbal inquiries about my age and an occasional disapproving glance complete with telephone inquiries to higher powers was I admitted to this free as bird place. I was now officially a camp member. My folks stayed to look about the camp and to have a light lunch before heading back to Mt. Healthy, Ohio. The time seemed to drag by as parental cautions, edicts and commands abounded. Eventually with faint tear and somber hand waving, the break was made. As the old Ford finally disappeared from sight down that dusty back road, I turned and once again savored the sight before me. My playpen had suddenly enlarged. But I was to soon find out that it was difficult to fly with seven-year-old wings.

Each cabin had two counselors and eight boys. That was fine. My brother was bunking in the same cabin with me. That was OK. The weather was warm and clear each day. That was delightful. The food was good and plentiful. That was satisfactory. What then was the problem? It dawned on me after the first day. The smiles and "hi buddy," were as thin as a politician's promises.

When it came to function as a healthy American boy I was shunned and avoided. Bad breath or B.O. was not the root cause. It was because I was seven years old and a runt in the eyes of my fellow campers. Even my brother tended to disassociate from me. I was last to be picked when choosing up side for games. No one sat next to me at mealtime. I had to find some one to sit next to. With nervous trepidation, I would ask if it was all right for me to sit there. A condescending grunt would be emitted that was taken as neutral consent. When the gaggle of boys would move across the lawns from cabin to commissary, from dinning hall to canoe livery, I was always in the rear. They seemed to be trying to out distance me or to elude my sophomoric presence. I wouldn't have it, as I double stepped and pushed into the ring of bodies when we stopped.

After three days, I was allowed to play some baseball after being chosen last again. They put me out in right field. *A safe place for an inept rookie.* In the ninth inning, the score was even between the two teams. A high, hard hit ball came towards me when I glanced over at the bench and noticed all the coaches had their hands clasped and heads bowed. I thought it was an unusual time to be praying. I saw the ball arching high and calculated that it would land far behind me. I turned and ran in that direction as sighs and then shouts came from my teammates. After an ambiguous run, I wheeled around to see the ball careening towards me, but at a slightly elevated angle. With one great leap into the air, with only my gloved hand extended, I stabbed into a void. With a thud and a sting, I knew with out looking I had snagged that elusive, freedom-seeking ball. Then I landed squarely on my two feet as the cheers of the entire baseball crowd reached my ears. My team won. With this one glorious moment tucked away in my record at camp, I was now accepted as another human being. But for how long?

It took several days for the swimming pool to be filled and chemically treated. Something about the pumps and parts also delayed its availability to the campers. We kept busy with baseball and other games. Canoe trips, long hikes, and craft times also made the time go by quickly. Therefore, it was the fifth day before we were assembled at the pool. It looked cold and clear. It also was quite large. The counselors made us use the buddy system and all had buddies except some of us who were small in stature. I was assigned an older boy to be my buddy, and we were told to stay in the shallow end of the pool until later in the week when our skills would be examined.

With a thundering shout of glee and surprise, we all jumped in. It was cold and shocking on our warm flesh.

My buddy and I jumped up and down at the shallow end and began to mix with some others as boys tend to do. He had on a blue swimsuit. Mine was red. I had to go after him and tell him of our buddy requirement to stay together. He eventually said to me that he was tired of the confines of the shallow end and would be back very soon. He was going to explore the deep. Away he went with a caution for me to stay put. Even with all the boys around me I felt lonely and out of place without my Buddy. I went to the side of the pool and edged toward the deep end to see how far I could go. My feet found a ledge along the pool wall that was about three feet down. I determined that holding on to the pool's lip at sidewalk level, and tiptoeing along this submerged ledge, I could advance towards the deep end and be reunited with my buddy who seemed to be doing the same thing I was doing. He was much farther ahead and was turning the far corner. I decided to increase my pace and was doing very well when I slipped. My hands lost their grip on a slippery painted line that went around the pool. My hands must have reached for and hit a wet slippery spot.

It was like a slow motion picture. I was descending into the water. The new angle of my body, caused by my released hands, could no longer support my weight in an upright position. My eyes were shut and all was quiet as fluid eatery hands began to gently draw me down to unknown depths. It took a few seconds to break through the embarrassment phase of another dumb kid stunt. What was every one going to say? How would my family and peers remember me? The seconds ticked away as voices and pictures flashed through my mind, much like fast forward on today's videos. At this point, there was a certain mixture of peace and panic that is hard to explain. Soon though, my lungs began to cry out in need, as the oxygen level waned away. The danger level moved on to a critical stage as I began to consider drastic options for survival. I hesitated a few more seconds, so certain someone, somehow would reach in the water and pull me out, with the comment that "we were only joking". It didn't happen.

I now was waving my hands side to side if I could touch the walls. With feet kicking, as a last desperate attempt to communicate with the outside world before going on to the next, *I opened my eyes.* I could see the sun's light rays shimmering through the liquid prison. It was pale blue with splashes of white, intermingled with wiggling swimmers bodies. All of a sudden, I was at peace again. Reunited with the world. Confidence in numbers. Not alone. As I gloried in my newfound surroundings, I noticed a stream of bubbles descending close to the right of me. In the front of this cascading array of hydraulic energy was a swimmer. I saw his back arched, as he prepared to return to the surface right in front of me. As he passed in his rapid ascent to the surface by kicking his feet and legs, I acted. Even though my air supply was exhausted and my lungs were prepared to inhale great volumes of water, I lunged forward and grabbed those passing, kicking legs. I was now going up even though several times the full force of a foot in my face was the cost. He was calling for help and kicking this unseen adversary as I broke to the surface. Gasping for one great breath, I also called for help. We were both pulled out and given artificial respiration. Soon I was giving the lifeguard a whispered account of what had happened to me. He acknowledged and whispered a brief sentence of explanation to my benefactor. "The kid was drowning and you pulled him by your legs."

Soon the crowd dissipated and I was left with a counselor who encouraged me with a promise that I would be swimming like a fish in a week. His promise was realized.

Those two weeks gave me much to ponder and remember. Good times. Good friends. Good lessons. The one thing I'll never forget is to keep your eyes open at all times to avoid tragic consequences.

The End

THE SHORTCUT

E VERYONE NEEDS OR TRIES A shortcut from time
to time. The regular way can become tiresome,
or time consuming or just boring. We look for shortcuts
on long journeys. We long for one when a task becomes
repetitive. When in a hurry, a shortcut beckons much like a
seductive courtesan luring us closer to the rocks with a song
of an elusive promise. "Around the Cape before the others."
An economy of effort and a badge of cleverness. Disaster
is always wished away and viewed with myopic eye. Like
life, the promise is not always fulfilled. The shortcut melody
comes to us when we are quite young and the strains can still
be heard when gray hairs grow sparse. Some shortcuts are
remembered and some forgotten. Some are incorporated into
the mix of doing and some are quickly discarded as burning
hot sips of coffee. Shortcuts can be accepted or rejected, as
they are only substitutes for the original, tried and true way.
To many of us when the shortcut is revealed it has a quality
of being a secret. A WAY that is not known by the more
common or less adventuresome. Only after much time and
copious tears does it become apparent that many shortcuts
have been known and avoided by those with higher I.Q's
than our own. All of these facts should not deter us from
seeking or experiencing shortcuts after some thought and
consideration. My shortcut here was a place and didn't take
the mind of a VCR programmer, or the savoir-faire of a
politician to enter in.

My friend was showing me the ropes. I had moved to
this little village in 1942. My father had built a new house on
the edge of town, about one mile from my new school. To get
to school, I walked East all along Adams Road to Harrison

Ave. Nice sidewalk. I passed middle class houses and well kept yards. On the corner of Adams and Harrison were several greenhouses and a florist shop. Just before that was an old vacant wood lot that would be important later on.

Now, I turned south on Harrison and continued up a slight grade, passing single-family dwellings until I came to the Christian Church of Mount. Healthy. Next to it was an alleyway and then the school yards started. First, the high school and then finally on the corner of Compton Rd. and Harrison was my new grade school. My friend, Dick G, was also a student there. We had met only a few weeks after I had relocated to my new house. I was nine and he was ten. We both rode bikes. My bike was a seven-dollar, solid wheel, cabbage green, eighteen-inch tire, girl's bike. Dick G. was an only child and sat upon his Schwinn, knee action, balloon tired, twenty-six inch, maroon beauty with pride and experience. Dick G. was a grade ahead of me and I was glad to know a mature fellow right off. When the weather began to change because of the coming of spring, Dick said one day, "Follow me, and I'll show you a shortcut to school." Since he came calling with his Schwinn, I grabbed my mongrel and away we went. The freezing and thawing of winter had dwindled down to a precious few occurrences. The snow had disappeared from all but the most protected areas. The morning was raw with cold but with the promise of spring in the air. It had dropped below freezing the night before. The frigid air carried our puffs of breath past our faces and to the rear as we moved along the concrete roadway. Mr. Adams would have been proud of his concrete ribbon, even though it was now punctuated with thick tar sealing bumps at its seams. My bones were rattling and my teeth were chattering as each bump was encountered with trepidation. I was following Dick on his metal steed as close as safely possible. All at once, he turned right off of Adams Rd, onto a driveway of one the middle class houses. I wondered if he knew who lived there and if we would be stopping to pick up another companion. When we had almost gone to the end of the private drive he suddenly veered sharply left and stood up to peddle and steer with more intensity. Before us lay a small strip of yard-grass, only 3 or 4 feet wide and then into sage grass and weeds that surrounded the vacant wood lot. Our bike tires easily found a tiny rut that began to weave its way into and through this dark, mysterious woodland. First, we had to negotiate up a small rise that propelled us into the very bowels of the wood lot. After obtaining this apex, we made a sharp right turn, continued along a ridge, across a small makeshift wooden bridge, and then slowly descended the hump to what looked like an old abandoned fire road. I was exhilarated. I could still feel the brush of tree limbs across my face and the rush of blood as the bikes traversed this roller coaster-like ride. My heart pounded as this fresh woodland air now filled my lungs after a moment of breathlessness. The trees stood like sentinels, with branches both forbidding and welcoming at the same time. Patches of snow lay in secret depressions that spoke of buried treasure and cave entrances. Clusters of bushes advertised secret hiding places for possible ambushes or even suitcases filled with money. I would never reveal this secret place and its location. We proceeded along the overgrown, unused alleyway until it spewed us out on one of the little back streets of my new village. That woodland part of the shortcut only lasted about two minutes, but its ambiance burned itself into my soul for all time. Lincoln Avenue, a short street of blue-collar worker's homes, was ahead of us now and ended about 100 yards further up a hill. At that point was an old barn close to the rear of the high school. Mr. Henshen's barn was barely standing but still held many winter repasts for his cattle. We continued beyond the hay barn and up a path to an alley that led to the back of the high school. Still peddling upward, we passed the rear of the Mount Healthy High School and came out on the playground of our grade school. One more short, steep incline that put us back on black top and then into the bicycle rack. Now we had a well-deserved rest for our two wheeled transporters and shank's mares. This saved only about five minutes of time but always gave the rider a sense of exploration and accomplishment. What a good way to start the school day.

Over the years my friendship with Dick G. rose and fell as circumstances dictated. I had to repeat the third grade and that put me two grades apart from my old neighbor. My little bike was not as dependable as his; therefore, I walked to school a lot. I always used the shortcut and so did my brother. We kept the pathway more noticeable and rutted by our frequent usage than when I first saw it, but the wood lot kept its charm and function. We always moved down the private drive on the far left, in case the owners would challenge us. We could then just jump into the high grass, move on up the weed choked hill and shout, "We're sorry!" It never happened that I could remember.

Since I "stuck" in the third grade, the teacher and my parents were all over me to take home a lot of books each night to do the Herculean amounts of homework required of failures. Each afternoon as school let out, my teacher would check to see that I was taking home the required number of bibliotheca to accomplish the assigned homework tasks for the night. School bags were for sissies and backpacks for students had not yet been invented. Each night I carried an armload of books to my home, where my mother would count and inspect each one with enquiries about the assignments for the next day. I could tell that parent and instructor were collaborating. It was an exasperating situation for a wee lad that had better things to do and more exciting stuff to think about. This went on through the fall and winter. I slowly became aware that the collaborating was no longer as astute as at first. Little hints. I could feel that I wasn't watched as closely, because the teacher only randomly checked on my homeward bound library and the parental questioning was ever more relaxed. With this lackadaisical security, I began to leave books that I didn't want to study from, under the little bridge in the shortcut. At home, I would explain of the fewer lessons, using complex explanations and coming inclement weather for the reason. All was well. The next day on my way to school I would retrieve the books from their hiding place under the little bridge and go on to school and make a show of them as I passed under the watchful eye of my teacher. What a plan. I now could listen to the radio in the evenings and spend time in the basement with my chemistry set. I was so very clever in my deception that I now left two books under the bridge and was thinking of three. One late January evening, after spending quality time at my chemistry lab, I heard the sound of thunder. I asked my folks why the loud noise in the wintertime. "I thought lightening and thunder was only for summer time storms." My father then told me about the January thaws, but I had never given them much thought before now. I ascended the stairs to my second floor bedroom and dozed off uneasily. I awoke the next morning to the gentle drizzle of a frigid winter rain. I stuffed a washcloth in my pocket so I could dry off my secreted books under the shortcut bridge. I also carried a belt to secure my books and would place the entire ensemble under my rubber raincoat. Off I went in the cold, wet morning with some foreboding of what I would find under the bridge. After all, the covering would protect them from snow as well as much of the rain and all I could do was say they got wet on the way to school in the damp conditions. Soon I was going up the private drive and into the sanctum of the forest's innards. Now at the bridge, my heart was pounding because of the abundant flow of water that was raging under the wooden crossing. I felt the place where I had put the books by laying down and moving my hand to the spot. The location was icy cold and under water. I could only feel the soggy, dead grass bed that had been the resting place of my future education. I felt on the other side and then all around in a frantic search for that which belonged to the school board. No books or bookmarks were to be found. I followed the rushing unanticipated stream to an aqueduct that disappeared under Adams Road and led to an unexplored ravine. The night's deluge had risen to my academic treasures and washed them away to oblivion. I had spent too much time in the shortcut. My knees where soaked and muddy and my mind was croaked and muddled. What was I going to do? What tale of woe could be believed? What kind of punishment if I fess-up? How much would it cost me to replace school texts? Schemes and subterfuge began to fill my head, trying to make a plausible answer for my dilemma. Too complicated I thought as I reached the old school house. Greetings were given to my friends as rote and I continued to move like a sleepwalker to my class. Like a condemned man, I approached the teacher's desk and soon was giving out carefully crafted accounts of my foolish activities. I knew very well that this would be the easiest of a two-part confession and trial. A few, "shame and Tuts, Tuts," with a promise of further evaluation was meted out and an unforgiving nod of the tutorial head encouraged me to take my seat for class. A three-dollar fine to replace the seven-year-old books that were "lost" eventually followed this. At home, the scenes were more painful as threats and vindictive voices were raised in tune with a month's, "on the property only," sentence summarily imposed. I lived through it all and never again hid books in such stupid places.

In the summer, I was daily going to the town's swimming pool. To get to the pool I need not use the shortcut. When I walked or was taken by Junie's (one of my friends on Adams Road, Clarence Jr. thus Junie.) mother to the pool we went straight up the road and across Hamilton Avenue towards the northern entrance to the city park. This route bypassed the shortcut, therefore I used it only occasionally in the summer. Upon returning to school in the autumn, I again made that woodsy walk my daily ritual. One afternoon when returning home from a learning experience at school, I noticed something out of the corner of my eye when traversing the raised ridge in the shortcut. I hadn't noticed it before because it blended into the foliage and could almost be called camouflaged. It appeared to be rectangular and almost solid in construction. It was out of place in this world of sun splashed, irregular shapes, and haphazard forms. A blemish on the sacred grounds. I approached the object of my youthful, curious, investigative, nature with care. Trying not to make a sound, I found myself arriving at the edifice that shouted out," summer shack in the woods," at me. It was empty. It was crude. It was an intrusion. It expressed a violation of my woodland wonderland. It was pathetic in construction and vulgar in appearance. The roof was made of various slabs of wood, different sizes, shapes, and lengths. The sides were a combination of slats taken from the Green House property and boughs cut and slashed from nearby trees. All was jammed unceremoniously in between two promising but now wounded saplings. A monument of wood butchers and forest thieves. Inside the crude lean-to, the grass was brown and trampled down. It cried out of over-nights and sleeping bags. Off to one side was a small circular stone fire-ring with the ashes of a once-friendly fire, rudely glaring out at me. Sounds could be heard in my imagination of sizzling hot dogs and the "yum, yum," of youthful voices devouring roasted marshmallows. The vulgar scene needed a special, altering touch. It didn't fit in and was an affront and an eye sore. An adjustment would have to be made. Looking all around the site to be certain of privacy, I deliberately found the areas of support and anchor by feeling with my foot. Casual, almost by accident, swings of my shoe caused a rearrangement of such proportions that for all intents and purposes the shack no longer was inhabitable. The wooden rubble lay before me like weathered matchsticks before an omnipotent giant. Then and only then, did a sick feeling come over me because of the dastardly deed that I had just committed. I looked guilty. I felt guilty. I was guilty. I left guilty but in the hope that I would not be found out for this senseless vandalism. With my eyes darting from side to side I left the scene of the crime with a certainty that someone was going to jump out from one of the vegetative hiding places and point an accusatory finger at me. Hope won out but it certainly died a thousand deaths first.

Several days later at school I found that some of the Lincoln Avenue boys were causally asking questions about the wood lot and my possible implication. "Did I still use the shortcut? Where was I last Tuesday? Did I see anybody messing around down by the green house? Ronnie, Tom, and Jack were all considered tough guys. My answers had to be careful and mixed with surprise when eventually they told of their camp and its destruction. Like a cross between a ballet dancer and a fox, I mentally danced around carefully and avoided all the set traps of persistent enquiries. Several times when returning through the shortcut on my way home from school I was sorely tempted to go back to the scene of the crime and try to reconstruct the shack. I held off for many weeks but finally got up enough courage to go one late fall afternoon. When I arrived at the spot, it was more terrible than when I had left it. Someone else had taken all of the material, scattered, and strewn it about so that all the kings' horses and all the king's men couldn't put wacky-shacky back together again. I was always saddened by my participation in this event. I learned that even a little destruction was usually the pathway for greater destruction.

The shortcut was used in all the seasons. The channel propelled me into the exciting world of uptown activities. Leaving behind the boring and catapulting me into the bubbling, via the oft used and idyllic shortcut, I looked forward to its daily utilization. It was there in the early morning, after school and now I would be using it at night.

Reaching an age when the Boy Scouts accepted young lads, I joined up with great anticipation of being away from home after dark. We went to the Grade School after supper on Monday nights, stayed until 8:30 or 9: 00 P.M., and then went right home. My brother, Bill, went with me for the first few times to make sure that I would be all right. He was a Scout long before me and knew the ropes. It wasn't long before I had made new friends at the meetings, came, and left when I decided, and not when my keepers saw fit to move. I left early and returned late, as the camaraderie was very welcome and fulfilling.

The autumn evenings were most memorable. Not too hot and not too cold. I left the house at about 6:00 P.M. and went to the meeting before Bill got started. We had outdoor meetings and ended with capture the flag. A great game of the mid-west that involved two teams and two flags. An imaginary line was drawn in the neighborhood and the flags placed at the most distant places practical in the neighborhood. This was usually one or two blocks apart. One team tried to capture the other teams flag without being caught or detected, and then would return to their side with the flag and win. It was great to stalk and hid behind bushes in the other teams territory. There, one could lay in wait until no one was watching the flag and make a run for it without being captured. When captured you were put in jail until freed by another team member touching the captive without being caught and returning to their side with immunity. Sometimes it was scary, as an opposition team member would catch you off sides by jumping out of some bushes or come from behind a tree and cry, "gotcha." DEAD MEAT, would then spend most of the balance of the night in prison, waiting to be released by a clever and quick team member. It was the greatest game I knew until spin the milk bottle came into my life. Better then hide and seek or even kick the can.

After a nights frolic of capture the flag we would occasionally go up-town and get a cola at the local drug store. Read the comic books and share some potato chips.

It would get late fast and I knew I had better head for home were Bill had probably been for sometime. I left the guys and headed out into the chill air of fall. Turning down Harrison Avenue I had the monumental chore of deciding to take the shortcut in the dark at this late hour. Before this night, I had always been with my brother or had taken the long way home where the lights were bright and the sidewalks wide. I walked fast and thought the same way. While walking past, the schools I had several opportunities to cut across to get to Lincoln Avenue and then to the shortcut. The last chance to do this was at Hill Avenue. It was late and I was certain that the minutes saved by using the secret path would ingratiate me with my parents. I would have to take control because I knew we all had some demons in our thinking process. Some are tame and some are wild. I was still trying to sort mine out so that there were more tame than wild. My feet found Hill Avenue and walking west I was soon near Henschen's barn and Lincoln Ave. Some of the houses were already dark from the inhabitants seeking slumber. I could now look down the street and see a great black void that hid the path that would take me the quick way home. Soon I was at the end of the pavement and began to adjust my eyes to the deep grays and suspicious blacks and purples that lay ahead. My feet landed quietly on turf and tuft as I left the light bathed land of the living and entered a quivering mass of unknown vegetation. Unknown because it never looked like this in the daylight or when an older brother was by my side. Deeper and deeper into the core I was propelled by excited feet. The branches of the trees moved and swayed in the night air giving me an arm-beckoning command to move with more speed. Whistling came to my mind and then to my lips as the stabs of outside light periodically penetrated the innermost bosom of the woods. Trees moaned in their bending and bowing. They creaked in agony as they stretched and scraped, trying to drown out my lip tunes. The whole scenario gave some validly to what my eyes where straining to focus upon. I could almost see headstones up ahead. That must only be the outline of bushes and maybe a stump or two. My heart raced, as I was now certain that some of the opposition team members would jump out now and take me captive, even though the game was over long ago. I stood still and didn't move. My throat was dry and even though I wanted to shout out that the game, capture the flag, was over I couldn't speak. My tongue was large and dry. I looked and looked, trying to determine what those shapes and noises really where. Those were voices, no, just the wind rushing through the grasses. Was that someone's head moving behind that tree? Probably not. No one would be here in the woods at this hour. Who would want me, anyhow? Just stay perfectly still for a little longer and try not to move even my eyes. They might see them if they looked real hard. I was getting cold. This was foolish. I could now see much better as my eyes became acclimated and accustomed to the minuscule light flickerings. I could now run along the ridge, out onto the driveway, be close to somebody's house, and cry for help if needed. I took a deep breath and scanned the area one more time and then began to run as if the demons from hell were after me. Some of the wild ones had got loose and some of their tame brothers had fallen off the wagon. Looking straight ahead, I made my feet guess where the path was located. My eyes sought out the opening at the end of the ridge and without feeling the snapping branches punishment, I soon exited down the little incline, across four feet of lawn and onto the driveway. Welcoming light came flooding from the street lamp and I felt safe as the sidewalk was now securely under my Keds. I spun around on the walk to take one last look to verify that no thing or no one was in hot pursuit. I knew I was alone but the turn about and peek was for the sake of my pounding heart and to return the escaped demons in their places. I continued my journey home at a double-time walk and was my old cheerful self as I entered the house. I was given the stern lecture for late returns with all of its warnings and threatening. I didn't hear too much because I was so thankful to be safe and sound once again on boring soil.

The shortcut provided cover in a town where small town eyes could be watching you at almost any moment. Occasionally I would use the shortcut for private purposes. Sometimes it was too far and too long to wait until one got home to avail himself of the special cover that was required when nature demanded. It was a good place to wait until one arrived before opening special notes that were received in school. It beckoned as a secluded spot to read one's first risqué' comic book.

I fell in with the Lincoln Avenue boys and found myself setting pins at the local bowling alley. A place where bad habits and bad language abounded. I tried my best to keep pure but was soon using a word or two that had not yet put in the dictionaries. I heard four words here that changed my life and caused me all kinds of expenditures and grief. Upon their utterances I would repeatedly answer in the negative. Eventually, "how about a smoke," caught up with my measured resistance and I acquiesced. I started smoking. "How about a beer?" fell into place. Too young to buy I would rely on some of the older guys at the bowling alley for smokes. When they would give me one or sell it to me, I would save it for later. The shortcut was the ideal place to stop and light up. It was a perfect place to rest a moment and drag deeply. The trees great boughs and their trunks easily covered my errant activities. The little stream was used to wash hands and lips to eliminate odors. Sometimes wild peppermint was available for breath control. I spent many hours in there, puffing away. It's a wonder that the trees stayed alive. Beers came later.

Adams Road was the recipient of a new family. They moved in about five houses away from me. At the same time, one member increased my class. I put two and two together when she said that she lived on the same road as me. She didn't say it to me but to the class when giving background information at the teacher's request. I was too shy to speak to her with out an excuse. She was pretty. Nice smile. I would like to know her better.

Watching her out of the corner of my eye when talking to the guys after school, I noticed that she too walked home from school. Some days I had a paper route and some days I would go over to a buddy's house to spend time after school. Some days I just watched Mary walk down Harrison Avenue and thought of the lost opportunity of walking her home. Several times, I followed her to determine that she was safe from predators. I had hoped she might look back and see me way off and then wait for me to catch up. No such luck. Each day she seemed to become more and more attractive. She sat on the other side of the room and it was awkward for me to look at her. I must get to know her. I tried to walk behind her more closely than before on the way home. Not too close. She may think I am too forward or pushy. She might scream and call the police or even worse, tell her mom about me following her.

I had a plan. I would go through the shortcut and time my arrival back on Adams Road at the very same second she would go by the private drive. It would have to be very casual and look like an accident. Nothing too elaborate. I would get to the tree sanctuary and wait for her to saunter down the road to the exact spot by the driveway and there make contact. I could peer through the trees without her seeing me. I could see her walking majestically for quite a distance. The first few times I positioned myself I only practiced mentally and made notes of time and distance. I finally had the mechanics down to a science and would have to begin the actual process. The desires had begun to stir within me because I knew of others with similar intentions in mind. To have or to have not. That is the question. I tried.

Each time my courage would abate at the last moment and with racing heartbeat and jellied knees I would become frozen to the spot. For a while, it seemed enough to just view her beautiful trek home and know I was as close as could be without becoming a first class idiot. One day a realization came over me that what I was doing was, in a sense, wrong. Real boys were bold and adventuresome. We could take what ever would come. On that day, I determined to come out from my hiding place and just say, "Hi." I moved into the shortcut with determined but esoteric resolve. There, she turned the corner and was walking as before, but now in my world of calibrated success. I now knew the exact spot where she would be when I must begin my causal walk out of the wood lot, on to the driveway and finally to that perfect juncture on the sidewalk where two would meet as one. I executed. She looked up at me and smiled when I was about fifteen feet away. Three long, excruciatingly yards, filled with a potpourri of emotions. Then I was there and said, "hi." She reciprocated and we joyfully walked together to her home. We repeated this walk together many times but always started from school and avoided the shortcut. No longer needed. We were good friends for years.

The shortcut is no longer there. It was bulldozed and a house erected on the sight of these recollections of days gone by. I only think of the shortcut on certain occasions and then with mixed musings. It seemed very important at the time, to me, to have such a place. It was the sight of various teachings and the place of several convictions. When we grow up, if we grow up, the need for a shortcut becomes very minuscule in comparison to the tried and true ways. Those ways invariably take us on the long way around and get us to the desired destination. Still, there is occasionally something within us to those that brands those ways "boring," and cries out with an impulse to once again visit the shortcut.

The End

THE INNARDS OF CCP ETC

I T WAS OLD. IT WAS misplaced. It was run down and decaying. It was dangerous. It was to be my academic home for a period of time for me to complete my studies to become a registered pharmacist.

It all started by me digging ditches and hauling manure at a nursery farm that raised flowers and other plants on the outskirts of my little home town of Mt. Healthy, Ohio. As a young teenager I had to work to provide for any of the extras in my life. Special clothing, shoes, or snacks were not furnished by my parental largeness. I spent a summer working in the hot greenhouses where the temperature would get up to 120 degrees or higher. We dug trenches and placed metal pipe in them and then covered the pipe with earth. Next came large sheets of canvas that were placed over this ground and wetted. Then hot live steam pumped into this system to kill fungus and weed seed etc. I maintained the boiler, and I had to examine the flowerbeds from time to time in the green house to ensure all was good. The heat was contained in the glass enclosures and that gave me a Turkish bath at no additional COST. Forty hours each week gave me about $10.00 per week clear. There had to be something better. A friend of mine was going to quit his drugstore job and if I got to the owner first, I could snatch up this desirable position and be paid 25cents per hour in the bargain. I was enthralled. The job opened up in late November, and I was hauling frozen manure by the wagonload out of farmer's cattle lots for the flower farm nursery when the opportunity came. I quit that job and was informed by a friend that I should go to the drug store owner's house on the next day after school. She was the widow of the store's namesake. Mrs.

McAteer lived out in the country about a mile and on the appointed day it began to snow. I watched throughout the day from my classroom. The snow piled up and the weather turned nasty. School was dismissed early because of the inclement weather. I put on my most determined look and boots to match and headed out the school door and with the call of good times in my ears from my friends They wanted to play pool or cards. I had to say no to their inviting calls because I was on a journey that would dictate all of my future life. I set out for the country. Through the snowy day and cold blustery windy opposition I persevered until at long last I spied my future employer's farmhouse. With my last bit of energy, I reached the porch and rang the bell. A surprised lady answered and invited me into the front room where she expressed astonishment at my presence on such a day. She was impressed. I was elated. She proceeded to interview me and soon gave me permission to start a trial period the next day at the store uptown. I left the snowbound house on wings of confidence and visions of entrepreneurial accomplishments.

The next day after school I reported to Jim Eich, the pharmacist in charge, who showed me to my duties that included but were not confined to soda jerking. In a matter of hours, I had mastered the art of jerking sodas, sundaes, malts, banana splits, cherry cokes, and flavored phosphates. It was a heady experience to learn all the secrets of the trade. Soon, I was ringing up sales, making out money orders, cleaning equipment of great importance, and making big batches of simple syrup. Jim Eich seeing my skills and expertise in all matters soon advised me to apply for apprenticeship papers so that if I chose I could enter pharmacy school at the end of my high school studies. All Pharmacists had to have at least 2 years of apprenticeship before he or she could be licensed. I applied and soon received my license for apprentice pharmacist. I worked in that store until the McAteer family sold it to Jewell McCollum.

I continued my employ there while attending pharmacy school. My good friend Rolla Eich was also going to attend the Cincinnati college of Pharmacy on John St. in Downtown Cincinnati.

After finishing High school, we both went to the college and took entrance exams and passed. It was run down and old but held knowledge and future for me that carried me over 40 registered years of trials and tribulation. That fall of 1952, we entered with high hopes in a class of 125 with other students from all over the country. Only about half every graduated 4 years later. My first assignment was to find a place to park my big four door green monster, Pontiac, as there was no room at the rear lot of the school. It was reserved for faculty and seniors. We found an old closed filling station lot up the street from school that was administered by an old black man named Cap. For 2 years, he faithfully performed his duty. We paid 15 dollars a month to park there and for old Cap to watch so that hub caps and other loose equipment would not fall off and disappear. It was well worth it.

The neighborhood had seen better days. The school building itself had been condemned, but by special permission, we could occupy it until the school merged with the University of Cincinnati in 2 years. It appeared to be an old high school that had been converted to the pharmacy college. The upper floors had stairs that held only a limited number of persons at a time. One stair that went to our algebra class was rated for only three people at a time. When more tried to ascend the spiral staircase, it would sway and creak. Occasionally we tested the stairs by having five or six on the structure at one time to see if the three persons limit truly represented the truth. The creaking and groaning indicated that the rule was just and righteous.

We were so poor that it came as a surprise in the big city when we found out that fat was supposed to have meat on it. We still packed our lunches and ate in the basement boiler room with the janitor. We would feed the rats that came around at lunchtime with scraps of food and watch them fight over it. The janitor was not too bright. When we talked about the "halogens; bromine, iodine, and chlorine, he was sure they were three sisters that lived down the street that sold their favors to the fellows from the better neighborhoods. Across from the school was a sign that stated *live worms for sale*, but we never saw any fisherman go in and make purchases of that kind. However, the place did appear to be busy.

On the third floor of the school was our chemistry lab and it overlooked much of the building across the street. Some of the boys noticed ladies scantily attired in the windows and took it upon themselves to throw coins across the street to that building with shouts of glee and encouragement. The boys must have assumed a business or some kind of special activity because the coins and shouts usually produced an increase in the girl's smiles. This happened several times until one day sirens and police cars came to that building and some ladies were escorted away with blankets about their persons into the waiting wagons. An indication that the sale of worms had reached a low point. Maybe drugs were the attraction?

The chemistry lab was the scene for many stories. We had large bottles of acid that we were told to be careful handling. One day one of the boys dropped a bottle on his pants and shoes. We immediately got him to stand up in one of the sinks were we began to pour water on the bottom half of his body to dilute the sulfuric acid. Soon, one of the professors came upon the scene and with much disgust sent our wet friend on his way home. Lucky lad. He went downstairs to the street below to await the bus, and we gave him catcalls from the third story windows as he stood there waiting at the school's bus stop just below our aerial viewing. As the bus pulled up and stopped, he gave one giant stride forward to get on the bus and he stepped right out of his shoes that had disintegrated down to the soles. He never even turned around and as the bus went on and he left those two soles right on the sidewalk below our window.

We also developed the shoot and wait water shot. I took a piece of glass tubing and heated it to melting point. By pulling it apart, cooling it and then breaking it, it made a piece of glass with an end a minuscule diameter. I then placed the larger end into latex rubber tubing and this was attached to a water spigot. If one turned on the spigot really fast and full, the water entered the rubber part of the hose with great pressure, then turns off the spigot, and aims the thin glass tube at someone clear across the chem. Lab, the result was compelling. The water would come out the tiny end with great force, but only about a foot long as the water turned off. While the water was careening through the air in an arc at some unsuspecting class member, I could remove the tubing etc. sit down, turn around, and nonchalantly talk to someone while facing in the opposite direction to the splashes. When it hit the person, they would look all around for a guilty face or obvious movement or displayed equipment and see none. They would then begin to look up at the ceiling, checking for leaks in the roof etc. It was great sport until others caught on and began to duplicate the skills.

Another great challenge of the chem. lab was the alcohol bottle. A one-gallon glass bottle was filled with pure grain alcohol so we could prepare many of the mixtures in pharmacy that required this pure, unique substance. Many of the boys saw fit to appropriate more fluid than was called for, thereby running out of that ingredient before all the class could finish their project. Student's off-key singing and awkward movements revealed this phenomenon about the lab as inebriation. When discovered, the professors devised a plan to place phenothalein, a clear liquid substance of great cathartic value, in the alcohol bottle thereby discouraging the indiscriminate consumption of the desirable free beverage. This produced a lessening of the sudden loss of alcohol from the great glass jug but increased dramatically the rapid forays of students to the bathrooms. Some times the exit journey was not fast enough thereby causing shame and humiliation to the boys who did not think ahead to bring clean undergarments. This scenario was soon played out as even the most adventuresome lads gave up and settled into complaisant submission.

The Chemistry lab was very interesting as was the above-mentioned pharmacy lab. All of this excitement took place in the same large third floor room. It might have been at one time a huge dormitory or gymnasium. At the end of the semester, we had to have all of our equipment checked back into the schools inventory and pay for any broken or missing pieces. A preceptor would stand by our desk area and read off the beginning inventory, and we would show the clean, secured item, and then after a check-off place it deep into the cavernous cabinet for next year's pupil. Flasks, beakers retorts, graduates and Bunsen burners, clamps, mortars and pestles of various kinds and sizes and on and on until the list was completed and the items not accounted for were tallied up and a statement for payment was presented to the hapless scholar. Some of us with. I.Qs over 100 and a semester filled with reckless abandon began to plot a system that would help our finances. The cupboards were locked with old locks that seemed to respond to many keys. We would check in one fellow that had the complete list of utensils, and then later when official eyes were not alert we would open it and transfer any needed equipment to the next fellow to be checked. Some flasks were probably checked in 10 times. We knew that most if not all the equipment would not be taken up to the U.C. Campus and would most probably find its way into the hands of some junk dealer so we were able to salve our consciences. I say fellow because we had only a few girls in our classes, and they didn't have a propensity to enter into our shenanigans. They were smart.

Messing with chemicals etc. caused a great stink one day when some one placed in our locker room a substance that shut down the entire school. We had only the one locker room for ourselves. It was filled with lockers and a ping-pong table. Because of the single game available to us on off class time most of us became very proficient at the game. The room was large and had two old iron radiators for warmth, and they had to go full blast to keep the frost out of the room on real cold days. Someone had noticed that a chemical had a special odor when in chem. lab and thought it would be pleasant to bring it down and share it with the boys playing ping-pong. Some fellows hogged the table so much that we thought maybe this would allow others a chance to play. The person put the substance (Ammonium Valerate) on the hot radiators and waited. Soon the room was filled with the odor that moved into the rest of the building with a vengeance. Within minutes, the entire building smelled like leavings of a long expired elephant that had been sick for days. The powers that were in control of the school but not their tempers announced angrily over the intercom that classes were suspended for the rest of the day. They also inferred that the culprits should begin to pack up their belongings and prepare for their permanent departure. Some of us left with sighs of regret and relief. Tempers soon cooled down so that no one ever left over the incident. We graduated in 1956

Before we left Cincinnati downtown and the college, we enjoyed it in special ways. We ate occasionally at the City Hall Cafe and even spent time in City Hall watching some of the court proceedings. It was a hoot to eat and rub elbows with the city's official and legal community.

We also had a place on Central Avenue that we frequented for lunch fare. A small deli permitted you to select what you wanted on your sandwich. (Izzy Cadets) A Bun-like affair that had sauces, meats, and cheeses of various descriptions. A kosher pickle topped the delight, and an amount that was always different each time was then collected. Izzy Cadet's became a special place to spend some time, as unique food was being prepared and served over the tall counter.

We also had a way to move through downtown utilizing many stores etc. thereby avoiding any inclement weather. One place served coffee and doughnuts and when we went out the back door we entered the next establishment such as Shillito's and so on until we reached the center of the city without going out into the weather.

One time we went to the Carew Tower and went to the observation deck and at 53 floors up we could imagine we controlled all we surveyed. Soon, we were playing with the elevator that was only on the top few floors, pushing buttons, and hiding from each other, sailing paper planes off the deck until adults arrived and caused us to cease and desist. Ultimately, we returned to the ground floor as grown up people and headed for the Gayety Theater. We had some long lunch hours that afforded us the luxury of going across town to the Gayety and yelling at the performers.

One of our High School members (Ray B.) could talk loudly as though he were Donald Duck and we would sit and watch him kibbutz with Blaze to the point she threw her strand of fake pearls at us because she was laughing so hard at Donald, that she could not continue with her performance. We had to leave there to get back to the real world and the humdrum.

We passed other theaters where on other occasions we would buy lunch, sit, and watch a movie. Once when watching a horror show in one of them, one of us dropped, our cola bottle (glass) and it began to roll down the cement steps (thunk!—thunk!—thunk!) under the seats. It was funny because it perfectly mimicked the steps of one of the on-film characters that were supposed to be tip-toeing toward an unsuspecting victim.

Soon, we were back in our classes learning all about everything. In 1954, we moved up to a new building on the U.C. campus teachers college. We had all new equipment and met new friends. Here, we bought box lunches for 25 cents to share with another student but didn't have to feed any to rodent critters. I met, Phyllis, my wife on campus, so the move to campus was a very good thing. They say these college years help form one's character for a lifetime. Therefore, they did. They helped me to appreciate all things and not to be fearful of change and where it will take you.

The End

THE SCAR

HARDLY ANYONE WANTS A SCAR but when one is produced, the inevitable thing is to live with it. The pain and apprehension of the cut or wound is eventually forgotten when bragging rights begin to show up. This wound or cut was acquired a long time ago and was not inflicted in a planned way. Our hero is the author of this story.

Growing up was a hard thing to do, but one must endure to arrive at that point of maturity when all young people must think there exists a Utopia. On the way up one must endure all kinds pitfalls and snares set by those that have gone on ahead. One of these snares was dating. The boy that enjoyed the company of his peers now begins to notice those once-despised entities called, girls. This affliction comes on young men at different times. My time came later than most. It was hurried by the acquisition of my first car. My friends had not yet been exposed to their own car yet so I became an object of a desirable conduit for double dating. This fact caused my friends to line up blind dates for old stodgy me. For the most part, they all turned out to be minor disasters.

Castle Farm was one destination for dates in my day. Other venues might be outdoor movies, bowling alleys, roadhouses, or cafes. The worst were dates lined up by my friend Jim. He had little taste, or vision concerning the principles of his date choices. This made it very difficult to relate to the girls since their visions of a good time were very different from mine. My forte was talking about studies at school, current events, new discoveries, and what the future would hold. Their discussions and interest were guy's physiques, curly hair, hot cars, and dancing. The talk was usually prompted by copious amounts of beer. In Cincinnati, a German oriented community, beer was thought of as food or a compliment of a good time.

When I was in collage the dating game was put on hold because the intense studies required for the courses we had to take, as well as the many hours that I was working to earn enough money to pay my own way concerning books and tuition. At the end of each day I was so exhausted there was no time to think of other pursuits. During my first two years of collage that I took, was in downtown Cincinnati. Only three girls attended our classes, and they were not my cup of tea.

When our college was melded into the University of Cincinnati, we were exposed to fresh bevy of charmers. My mother insisting that I join a fraternity that my family had been associated for years complicated the scene. This new class of guys tried to line me up with sorority girls called Greek girls. They had the reputation of being loose and easy. This caused me no end of anxiety because my shyness and my standards for dating someone that would disappoint me for marriage material.

At the insistence of the fraternity's officers, I agreed to go on a blind date. This anticipation was very intense because I was led to believe I should perform in a certain way so that I could relate in detail all of the happenings to the Greek body of sex starved men or boys. I was prepared by some of the members to help me overcome my fears and shyness. This only increased both of those emotions. I was not told who the girl was or what collage she was in but only that she was Greek on campus had a good track record??

When the evening finally came around, I had some members accompany me to a sorority house where we were introduced to a bevy of young ladies. I was told to expect one of the girls to be my date that night. After much drinking and circulating around the room, a young girl came up to me and informed me that I was her date for the night. She was tall and willowy and with dark hair and dark eyes made up like an Egyptian and not a Greek. I found my Greek buddy, and the four of us went to my car, a 1940 four door Pontiac sedan, I called the green monster. This car became a topic of discussion for a few minutes with caustic remarks about its age etc.

The green monster was old but roomy and comfortable. Those hot cars girls liked so much were small and rode like hay carts. I was proud of my car because I had rebuilt a lot of the parts, including the engine. The monster had been repainted, and body putty put into all the seams. The muffler was cool with an extension that gave it a purr in low RPM's. We rode around for sometime before I was told to head for Castle Farm. Tooling through the traffic, I noticed tall and Willowy was sitting next to the door in a Ho-hum attitude. 'What fun this going to turn out to be,' I thought as we pulled into the gigantic parking lot. At that time, I noticed we all were puffing on cigarettes, and the car smelled like the bottom of an ash try. Throwing away my cigarette I placed a new one in the corner of my mouth in jaunty manner to show how grown up and cool I was. It didn't seem to impress anyone as tall and willowy led the way out with me trailing slightly behind the gaggle.

We entered the mammoth building, paid for our entrance fee, and found a table in the back of the room. Sitting down we all ordered exotic drinks to bring us back to a giggly state of existence. Smoking and drinking until our bodies were sufficiently poisoned, we all tried to dance with each other as clumsy patrons. This condition was not something I really wanted. It just seemed to be the thing that college kids did to feel more grown up and cool. My date only danced once with me, as my moves were stiff and uncoordinated. She (Roz) found a few loose boys around our table area to dance with. Of course, it was with my permission. She asked in a very positive manner. (May I dance with this fellow while you sit out this fast one?) She had told me that she was going to be in Police work, hoping to be a detective one-day. I was not impressed. Therefore, it went to the chagrin of my Fraternity Brother. When the evening finally ended for us, we agreed it was time to leave, and so we did.

Getting into the green monster I was certain it was time to go since we had snacked and drank ourselves to the point of silliness. I soon found I was wrong.

"Let's go for ride and find a place to park," came a suggestion that had a slightly commanding sound. The tenor voice came to me with a smattering of giggles from the back seat where two thought as one. In the front with me came only a deep sigh or resignation.

"Where to," came my retort in my most obeisant voice. A slight pause came as the back seat though about my request.

"Oh. Just drive around until I tell you where to stop," came an all-knowing answer of experienced dimensions.

Driving around I was aware of some shifting and soft whispering from the back seat as I endured the iciest of Arctic air in the front seat of the green monster. I didn't care that the evening was a waste of time as well as a drain on my meager funds. We found a parking lot where a stop was made for only a short time when I was directed to drive the people back to the various homes or Sorority houses. After my Greek brother and his date had been left off, I took tall and willowy Roz, to her apartment. On the steps, we paused for a moment, each wondering how the night would end. I thought I might get at least a good night kiss so I pursed my lips and tried to get close to her face. It didn't work.

"If you would get out of the hole you are in, I might give you a good night kiss," said tall and willowy with a certain acerbic edge.

Those words cut me like a knife. The comment validated all that had gone before and prophesied all that would yet come. I knew I was small for I had small feet, small hands, small nose, small hands, small everything.

So, there it was. A slash across my heart that has left an enduring scar as a constant reminder of whom I was. That scar now is small but it does crop up from time to time with near catastrophic results. The negative it produces must be put in its place. After many years of a successful marriage and blessings from the Lord, I seldom see the scar or recognize it. I must admit those words long ago had burned as well as cut. The burning was like a branding iron, now only to remind me that what we say, how we say it, and to whom we say it, can a most important sentence for the recipient. I would like to think these words will erase any scars that might be bothering the reader for I have now just noticed my scar has completely disappeared.

The Beginning of scar less days

The End

HIKER BOB

H E CAME INTO CAMP LIKE a mountain wind, with a black beard, piercing eyes, legs like tree stumps and a growling stomach. We were soon to be touched by wind, words, and wiliness. This man appeared to be one modern day outdoorsman, eating only leaves, grass, twigs, and mushrooms.

Uncle Walt first encountered hiker Bob on the Laurel fork north wilderness trail. When I initially saw Walt in deep and intense conversation with Hiker Bob my intention was to dawdle a while until this fishing diversion had passed. The two did not part. Not to be considered rude, I lazily fished for trout on the Laurel River until I was quite near and noticeable. Finally, I moved onto the trail and causally eked my way towards the two conversationalists. When I approached, each took a deep breath and paused long enough for introductions. Bob was the hiker of note. I was introduced as UNCLE DICK and I replied to Walt as UNCLE WALT. The names stuck with Hiker Bob throughout his long and interesting visit. Walt soon ended his dialogue with Hiker Bob as I began to head back to camp. The outdoorsman followed me like a puppy, giving observations, opinions, and self-history out loud to me and the trees.

We followed the trail and soon came to the first set of campsites where I gave a glowing appraisal of all the attributes and advantages. These sites had an outhouse close by and was close to the stream. A table and pavilion enhanced the well-manicured lawn. A Water pump was in evidence. A fine place for hikers and campers like us to bed down for the night. The area was deserted; a feature that I was certain would appeal to Hiker Bob. He took off his giant backpack and set it down as he surveyed the scene. Soon the words that sent chills up and down my spine were uttered. It was as though the other shoe fell or like falling in the chill deep waters of the Sinks of the Gandy. They were barely audible, but I discerned their meaning at once with much trepidation.

"Where is your campsite?"

Like a hound dog sniffing the winds, Hiker Bob had found a tasty morsel and was not about to give it up to some pretty scenery. Moving with the convictions of a Mountaineer with a Sherpa guide, Hiker Bob took up his heavy pack and giddily said, "Lead on uncle Dick."

Hiker Bob followed me back to the last campsite; the one we occupied. As we trekked through the campgrounds, I again pointed out all of the amenities and advantages of the State prepared sites to Hiker Bob. He would have none of it. At last, we came our site, the last one in all of the area. Bob licked his lips and declared, "This is wonderful." He could set up his tent only a little way into a pine thicket about a stone's throw from ours.

In a short time, Hiker Bob had set up his tent in the thicket and occasionally eyed our site for activity. We continued to do our usual things around the campfire. Bill and Billy from Cleveland, Ohio, and also Connie were in chairs just lounging and living the good camper's life. Connie is Bill's father-in-law and Bill is Uncle Walt's son. Billy of course is Bill's son and Walt's grandson. One of Walt's other sons, Keith, was also on the trip with his daughter, Candice. When Walt returned from his foray into the wilderness fishing for trout (the reason we were on this trip) we were all together with Hiker Bob permanently ensconced in the family circle. Bob was talking with an air of dedication and confidence that boggled the mind. There appeared to be no subject that was foreign or unknown to Hiker Bob. He was able to lecture about mushrooms to far away countries with a depth of knowledge that kept some of the boys up until the wee small hours of the morning. Bob seemed to be present at all times, most especially at mealtime. Hiker Bob had a broad forehead, a black beard, and eyes lively and yet haggard. His hat was like an inverted navy gob cap. His shirt was the color of dirt and for good reason. A few holes in it made it look like a designer garment. He wore shorts that were frayed at the leg holes. They also howled out for soap and water. When close to our guest it was easily noticed Hiker Bob could use as bath or start growing his own mushrooms on his person.

In the mornings, we would begin to prepare campground savory foods that even today makes my mouth water. While making the fire, we didn't see Bob. While chopping wood we didn't see Bob. While peeling spuds or making pancake batter, we didn't see Bob. While cooking the victuals, we didn't see Bob through our smoky and stinging eyes. When we began to serve up the delicious food, then we saw Bob with his tongue licking chops and growling stomach. It was a sight to see. At the end of each meal, Bob vacuumed up all the leftovers with sounds of delight. A few utterances of appreciation and approval were to be heard if one listened closely.

It soon became apparent that Hiker Bob had found a home and was content to exchange talk and spurious information for the warmth of the fire and the bounteous amount of available food.

Hiker Bob was gregarious to a fault. He liked to be with people when not alone on the trail if the conversation was stimulating and the food ample and goodly prepared. He was able to add to any information one of us offered up for his benefit. We quizzed him on snakes and solitude, bugs and bears. He was a veritable fountain of information. I am sure this is how he felt he was repaying us for our camaraderie and calories.

Bob was a little shaky on morals, having explained he had a girlfriend for seven years who had recently left him for better family opportunities. Bob did not appreciate her biological clock running out. His philosophy was to learn and hike or was it hike and learn. Not much, earn or give in that kind of existence.

Bob stayed, talked, and ate for several days. Bill, Billy, and Connie all left for Cleveland. Bob stayed and ate. Candice was enthralled by the visitor and asked him many questions in between riding her bike around the campsites trying to avoid Saltwater Chubb(an irritating little boy from some far off campsite.) and locating cake and chocolate from an old couple at the other end of the campground. Candice had achieved Cave Master status on this trip by going both ways through the Sinks of the Gandy. Pretty good for a six-year girl or is she five?

While Keith and Candice packed up to leave, we had to decide what to do with food that was partially consumed. We left many partial food containers for evaluation and selection. I kept some and put them into my camper. The table as filled with these opened containers of food items when we told Bob he could have any that he wanted. His eyes lighted up like 4th of July fireworks, His mouth drooled, and his fingers twitched as he moved to the table and began to accumulate the offerings of his newfound family. Peanut butter, flour, jams, breads, and condiments all began to be placed in their new home. (Bob's Backpack.) It was a sight to behold. Such joy and satisfaction played upon the hiker's face. He worked with the food with the artistry and intensity of a concert pianist. Each item was carefully wrapped or folded or bagged and placed in a duffel on the top of Hiker Bob's Pack. In just a short time, all visible signs of foodstuffs were gone and in its place was a wide and happy grin upon Hiker Bob's weather worn face. Keith and Candice left. Hiker Bob stayed. Uncle Walt, and I tried to be civil while Bob was still in our campsite but finally I excused myself to go to the stream and take a bath with soap. This was an exercise that

Hiker Bob should have taken several times over. We all had tried to stay upwind from the world traveler.

After I left and began to bathe in the stream I kept looking back to see whether Walt would excuse himself, thereby giving Hiker Bob the unmistakable sign of that the party was over. Soon, Bob left and Walt came over for a cleansing in the stream.

When Bob had left and we both had bathed in the water with soap; it became quite apparent that the area had been cleansed from all kinds of smells and objectionable matter.

We returned home that same day anxious to tell of the times and tales of Hiker BOB.

The End

OLD SUNNY

OLD SUNNY WASN'T ALWAYS OLD, but he was always sunny. My only daughter and her best friend were in one of those shopping centers that have everything. They were young girls in that 14 or so age bracket. That time of life when emotion and reason are like oil and water. So what if we already had a dog. So what if it meant feeding and caring for a living thing for years to come. To have and to hold in sickness, health and when barking. Therefore, who cares if long and intensive training are required to instruct it to relieve itself outdoors and not indoors on Mothers favorite carpet is needed. No thought is given how to avoid chewed up slippers, shoes, rocking chair rockers, TV electric cords, cherished antiques, and other insignificant personal property. The cerebral activity of teenagers in this arena of thought, concerning responsible long-term commitment is near the zero range.

Two young girls, gaily walking down the mall without a care in the world, come face to face with the cutest, most cuddly of creatures, God ever put on this Planet. With noses pushed hard against a glass window, separating their boredom from their joy, they stare. Their minds reeled with the thoughts of them, romping through fields of clover with their canine companions on flower fragrant spring days. Mental pictures flashed in their brains of them, showing their school chums these wonderful additions so recently acquired. A pal to roll with on the rug in front of a roaring fire in the family room on a cold winter's night. The pictures came faster now that two of the wiggly, squirming masses came over and pressed their black noses up against the separating glass and seemed to smile in agreement. Eyes met, hearts melted, bells rang, as quivering lips blurted out, "let's go inside and see how much they are". Soon it was puppy against flesh, in that special furry way. The final, clinching act is when eyes meet again without glass restraint and puppy tongue reaches out and finds the teenagers face for that electrifying moment; that eternal bond of affection that nothing on earth or in the sky, can alter or remove. Hands fumble and lips tremble as the contract is made. Old filthy lucre goes over the counter one way and eternal love and affection comes the other way into eagerly awaiting arms that will never give up this treasure. The deed is done.

I was working long hours and would come home dead tired. Phyllis, my wife, would have a nice supper prepared. Afterwards I would retire to the TV room to put my feet up, read the paper, and watch some television. Phyllis came in after a very special dinner one night and broke the news to me that Linda, our teen-age daughter, had purchased a puppy. It really was no new news to me. I had seen a box in the far corner of the kitchen. The little sounds and the big smells revealed to me quickly that a new creature was in the house. I took a long breath and began to think of all the ramifications of such an event. Poor Phyllis. I commenced to spew forth all the reasons for the impossibility of this adventure. We already had a dog. A good little house-broken beagle that was everybody's pet. Linda was too young to assume such a long-term responsibility. We were short on cash to feed an extra mouth. We all worked or went to school so no one would be home to care or train a new animal. On and on went the reasons until I finally stated in the usual strong paternal manner, "that the puppy would not be in this house when I came home from work tomorrow." I was certain that would settle it because Phyllis always listened and responded to the letter of the request when I was serious or intense. I was most confident that would settle the puppy episode for good. I was relieved and yet distressed that occasionally a father had to be so harsh on his loved ones. It had to be done! It was part of the dog eat dog world.

The next night as I entered the front door with some trepidation my eyes searched out for boxes as my nose was lifted a little higher for advantage to detect the puppy thing's possible presence. It was nowhere to be seen in the house. My olfactory senses were surprised to find no traces of puppy. I was awed with a sense that my mission of severity in the path of permissiveness had been accomplished. I was after all, the captain of my own kingdom. The evening dinner was served and eaten with no hint of the events of the day concerning puppy. Pepper, the beagle was greeted by all with the usual familiarity and affection. All seemed back to normal. I eventually retreated to my after dinner spot in the TV. room and the relaxed position of my recliner chair. I was reading my paper when I heard it. Little clicking sounds that occur when nails tap on hard wood floors.

It had better not be a puppy dog. My word was law. How could they not obey? Later I was to find out that the little dog was not in the house as I had ordered, but had been quartered out in the garage. After all, any one with an ounce of brains knows that out in the garage is not in the same as in the house. Surely, my word had been obeyed.

I looked over my up raised paper to see a little black body full of fur that embodied a puppy. Little feet prancing on the floors with head slightly turned to the side so as to not miss anything of sound or sight. He stops and looks at the head behind the newspaper. He doesn't move a muscle. He stares back at the red faced head of the household and gives no quarter. A long moment ensues. It is pregnant with scenes of the future of both participants. Good days. Bad days. Training. Scoldings. Licenses. Collars. Dog houses. Nights of Barking. Surprise messes. Time-sharing. Even Christmas gifts. All seemed to fade and disappear when the black fur began to wag a little tail and seemed to grin as he carefully made his way into the sanctity of that room and my heart, with a little help of a teenage hand just out of sight. As I leaned over to pick him up, I knew that without any hesitation that we would be pals for a lifetime.

It wasn't long before I was building a new doghouse out of the old one that Pepper didn't need. The boards were heavy. Double thick in many places. Two by fours and thick planking, topped off by real tar and pebble roofing shingles. It took one of my sons, Mark, and me to move it about the yard. The puppy took the name Sunny very quickly and started by obeying my commands on about every seventh occasion. He had a fine appetite and cleaned up his dish every time. He grew and he grew. He learned to roll over and play dead. I could put food on the floor and he wouldn't touch it until I snapped my fingers. He was a fast learner. Maybe it was the socks and shoes that he ate that made him smart and grow so fast. Wood became part of his diet from time to time. Chair legs were not safe. The antique rocker did lose part of one of its rocker on one unattended hour. Electric cords became ragged looking, as did my nerves. "This dog is going to be an outside dog," I roared.

The first night out side the little fellow proceeded to sing and howl like a wolf or banshee. It was not the only time neighbors would inquire by phone as to the health and future of our canine critter. Sunny ate table scraps and seemed to grow even faster. His coat always stayed the same even though at first we thought after puppy hood it might change. He always was furry and took on the look and countenance of a bear. Because he was so much bigger than our beagle. I often called him Moose. As I recall he had a white patch on his breast and one or two of his feet also had some small amount of white. He liked to jump straight up on all fours when he was excited or happy. He would run around our house outside, several times before allowing you to pet him after I let him off the chain. Now fully grown he wasn't over thirty pounds but he was a dynamo of energy. I attached his chain to the heavy doghouse and he proceeded to yank and pull on the chain until it broke. I kept on buying dog chains. He kept on breaking them. I bought thicker and thicker chains until I got to the size they use on logs. A log chain. Then the collars starting breaking as he pulled against the new chains. I kept buying thicker collars until they were the size used for German Sheppard's. We even had him fixed to slow him down. This along with the stronger constraints was our last hope. This combination of big chain and thick collar now provided this black ball of fury a new opportunity. I chained him to his extra heavy dog house that took two of us to move.

During the night, a strange dog or other critter must have come into the yard. Sunny gave out the alarm. Incessant barking soon gave way to primal howling upon my vocal urging out the window. Eventually the neighborhood returned to some degree of peace. When I awoke the next morning and looked out the window I was aghast to see that great and heavy doghouse at the other end of the yard. MY first thought was that some irate neighbor, had in the middle of the night, pulled that dog and his house to the far end of the yard and silenced Sunny by some spurious means. Calling to the dog after I went outside I was relieved to see him unharmed and happy as ever. That evening, with the help of one of my Sons, we dragged that dog box back to the side of the house. There it stayed for several weeks until one moonlit night I heard Sunny with his ever-present built-in alarm system. Barking in that special way that indicated a stranger on the premises. I looked out the back window and saw an alien dog slinking around and making a general nuisance of it. Sunny was now lunging with great power, towards the intruder making that chain taunt. With each and every lunge he made the dog box move and thereby telling its own story of yard movement. It was hard to watch. Each lunge looked like it would break his neck. The stranger noticed the ever-advancing king of the area and finally departed. However, not before Sunny had moved that cumbersome abode of his half way across the yard. Now I must anchor that box by some ingenious means to keep it from wandering all over the neighborhood. I tried stakes in the ground. No avail. I put those corkscrew anchors made of steel that one had to screw into the ground to keep it from pulling out. Attach him to it and don't worry about the doghouse. Forget it. He pulled them out of the ground with lunges and lurches of only about two weeks duration. We finally used trees to fasten the chain. It worked. Now raising Sunny would be easy.

We moved the doghouse around the yard to give it a chance to regain itself. One dog in one area made the grass turn to bareness. We then used the box to attach the chain to, hoping the dog had forgotten that the chain could give a little. Linda had given Sunny a great big red bow for his collar because of the Christmas Season. The dog now spent about half his time in doors and the other half out of doors. He needed to go out. He was taken out and secured to the chain and box for his breath of fresh air. His nightly antics hardly even raised an eyebrow anymore. The next day we observed that dog and chain were gone. The thought occurred to all of us that with a chain still on his collar he was at greater risk than usual. That dog with a red bow and a log chain trailing behind would be easier to spot than ketchup on a white suit. Not so. We spent days looking to no avail. My wife Phyllis put ads in the local paper and also told all ours friends to be on the look out. We formed teams of people and walked the railroad tracks. My thought was that he headed for the woods and got his chain wrapped around a tree. Therefore, I spent some time in the woods around our own part of town. Phyllis even contacted the animal shelters, dog warden, and every other agency we thought might help. In this process, we luckily came upon a friends lost dog and saw that they were reunited. When hope had reached, its lowest ebb Phyllis heard that someone in the Hospital where she worked saw a dog tied to the flagpole in the front area of that Hospital. After some detective work and a few phone calls we found that the person that took Sunny home, had set out on a trip and the dog refused to stay in the vehicle. That person in turn farmed out the dog to another friend so he could go on his trip. The phone number of the friend was obtained and upon our arrival to that person's house, we were reunited with one happy black nosed dog. Tears and wagging tail made the entire exercise one that would be told to Grandchildren in the years to come. The whole tense situation proved one thing conclusively. The collar was rugged enough. The chain was strong enough. The box was anchored enough. The eye screw that was mounted in the box was the weak link. He pulled on it until it was pulled straight. Off to the hardware Store again for a screw eye as thick as my thumb. Strong enough to pull a car. I hoped it would work. However, I really wasn't sure.

Sunny continued to be a best pal to each one of the children. The children, one by one left the nest and went their various ways. The old dog stayed at the homestead and was a pal to me the longest. We planted the garden each year and worked through the summer until harvest time. Sunny was trained to stay in the yard and not run way. He had attained a certain maturity. He also spent all of his time in the house because of his perfect house broken manners. Even after we returned from eight hours of work or travel, there were no accidents. We walked in the woods across the street and saw the trees turn to golden yellows and brilliant oranges. We shared the couch through good TV. and bad. He always met me at the door after work and greeted me with his wagging tail and a dog faced grin. A few jumps up for kisses and then out the door to run around the yard checking for the scents of friends and strangers. When he had finished going over every square inch of the yard he would whine to get back in the house to check his food bowl for goodies.

His slow-down came slowly but was only noticed as a real handicap at the last. He began to move much slower and have accidents from time to time. We thought maybe we were away too long. A dog at fifteen years old it was be expected to some degree. The whole merry go round was coming to a halt. No one wanted to recognize the symptoms and the conclusion.

I found that the accidents were so frequent that I made a new box in the garage and bought a bale of straw to keep him clean and warm. We now kept Sunny in the garage because he had a habit of running off and forgetting where he was. Neighbors would call and comment and then I would go get him and carry him home. Even though cold weather was here, he kept comfortable and dry in the garage. Now when I came home I would have to get him up and help him to walk to get started. His soulful eyes would look up at me and he would appear embarrassed. They seemed to say, "I'm sorry." After a while, he was able to navigate pretty well. I bought all his favorite food. Dog food in a can that contained meat. Instead of cheap, dry food. At first, he bolted it down but after a while, even this delicacy lost its appeal. Through all these changes, we thought about going to the vet, but no one had the courage to make the final decision. It was Christmas time and we all wanted to be merry. Finally, on the 30th of Dec. we could no more prolong the inevitable. Calls were made to the vet and he was taken by his mistress and Phyllis to the vet's for the humane answer for old dysfunctional dogs. I had earlier in the year dug a grave out by the old garden. A place that old Sunny had watched me plant many seeds that later would grow up and produce vegetables. I had kept it covered so he wouldn't notice it as he made his last few rounds of the yard in late autumn. They brought Sunny home wrapped up in a shroud. We went to the grave and uncovered it to find that the late December days had brought enough precipitation to cause it to be filled with water. With a bucket, I began to bail out the water. We couldn't put our friend in that cold wet place. With cold hands, wet knees and tear laden eyes I couldn't continue. My youngest son,

Scott finished the difficult process. We lowered Old Sunny into the ground and said a prayer and sad farewells. Scott and I covered him over and I cried the tears that spanned 15 years. Now I knew why I had fought so hard not to pick up that little black ball of fur 15 years earlier. I'm glad I did. Old dogs never die they just dim away.

The End

HUMPTY DUMPTY
(equine version)

I T WAS A COLD AND wet day. The kind that if you had the money and the influence, you would never buy one. Walt's farm was buzzing with activity. Just like a western omelet, it was taking on new flavors at every turn. Keith was in the barn with hammer and saw. Much as an artist attacks a great block of granite with only a vision in his mind, Keith was rearranging the barn. His sculpture was solid wood horse stalls with wider gates and heavy wire screening over the windows. The construction must be strong and precise because of the new registered inhabitants, soon to be housed. Stallions. Thoroughbreds. Fine stock. High horse flesh.

A great load of rough poplar boards was situated by the driveway. Measurements were taken by the sculpture and transferred to the woodpile. Boards were laid one on top of the other, and the rule placed on their surface. At the proper length, a nail scratch line was made. Grabbing the chain saw, the artist fires up the engine and commenced to cut all five boards immediately. Like a chisel against granite the wood gives up it, resistance and chips fly as the lumber falls away, one by one. Five boards, perfect size, ready to take their place in the great hall of champions.

Each of the planks is hammered into the waiting oak frame. Great glassy eyes watch every move as nostrils flare from time to time. The great stallion King gives out challenging whinnies to notify the humans of his presence and to declare his mild discontent. A nicker from King has depth and meaning. Even in an adjacent stall, the king knows that the construction-taking place is in the best interest of all the players and actors, including himself. The building continues at a furious pace because of the new arrival tomorrow of Dancer. This colt is the birthday present of Billy, a young man who will grow with the gift. Much has been accomplished as the light begins to fade into night. The two orphan calves begin to bawl for their evening bottles of milk. Soon, two giant bottles of warm milk come into the barn, accompanied by the calf's nouveau mater. Caryn is soon managing the nourishment-giving chore that is concluded in a matter of minutes. Two empty containers are all that Caryn has for her efforts. A few butts in the seat, and sad calf eyes rolling, ends the scene. Time for bed.

The next day began as a repeat weather wise. The manicure man came to trim the hooves of the great beasts and the pony. One by one, the equine inhabitants presented their feet to the man with the apron. Some with more hesitation than the others. As I held the heads of these great weighty animals, I was hopeful that the MAN didn't bite into the quick. He didn't. All turned out well. The day was filled with city parades with Candace majestically ensconced upon an open-air automobile. Sweet Lou giving encouragement to the filming of the event. Carnival activities mixed with food of the same ilk. Brian was visited in the hospital, where the food was bad and the nurses weren't. New members of the clan arrived and soon found their places in the West Virginia topography. Rick stayed thin by running after Logan. In the evening the new colt, Dancer was presented to Billy along with the singing of the birthday song. This festive event was followed with pineapple upside down cake with or without milk.

Sunup brought hope and determination. The owner-manager-ruler and lord of the ranch soon was home and made his intentions known. "It was time to saddle up King and ride him. He hadn't been handled or ridden for a very long time. I'll have to show him who is the boss!" Walt concluded this discourse by fetching the great stallion. Bill put the cinch in position and readied the great horse for the equestrian skills of King's new owner. Days of anticipation mixed with years of experience clothed the horseman as he mounted the frisky stallion for the first time. For one frozen moment, the picture of rider and horse was a vision of beauty for those of us watching. The animal standing erect with muscles aroused in the morning light, his gleaming chestnut coat reflecting his youth and vigor. The rider, erect in the saddle and at attention. His eyes glued on the head of his mount to monitor the slightest motion or twitch to signal any sudden change in stance or circumstance. The only thing missing in this poetic and timeless sight of man and beast was background music.

It all happened in a second of time. However, to the enthralled viewer it passed in unbelievable slow motion. It was like a surprise birthday party that came a day late. It shouldn't have happened. It reminded me of the time I went to the best restaurant in town and ordered their best steak. When it was served, it was dry and hard to cut. It tasted rancid, and the portion was small. Ready to explode with comment and action I noticed a sign on the wall that put the whole scene in a sort of fantasyland. It paralyzed my reaction. The sign belched forth its message loud and clear. If you don't like your steak, please just leave quietly. My eyes couldn't translate properly what they were seeing now, with steed and horseman.

King, with electronic speed made three motions immediately. Up from a sanguine stance, as though a volcano erupting. A sideways lunge that was reminiscent of the flick of perspiration cast from the brow of a sweaty, winning athlete. Lastly, a bolt that propelled all movement and bodies in a forward thrust that verified to the rider he was mounted atop a lightening thunderclap. All was fastened with only two of the necessary three ingredients needed for success, confidence, and skill. The other requirement soon presented itself as woefully lacking. Preparedness. The belly cinch was giving way as its function was being tested to the limit. It slipped. The saddle moved. Off and into the air came the recipient of this minuscule flaw. It was a sad sight. Flesh and bone that no longer fitted into its proper space. Suspended in air, with arms flailing for a grip in the unobtainable breath of surprise. Gravity pulling ever harder and faster as the mass of protoplasm began its downward journey. Bones and joints, muscle and sinew, nearly 60 years old, made millisecond adjustments in midair. Tucking his arms to his sides, pulling his legs up to his waist and with Jesus in his heart, he waited for the rushing conclusion of falling off his beloved horse. It is not the fall that one dreads, but it is the sudden stop. And sudden stop he did make. Walt landed on the hard packed gravel with a thud and then an unexpected bounce of two inches. It was painful to all of us. He only stayed in that sprawled down position for one second as we ran to see whether he was hurt in any way. He immediately got up and brushed off himself with only a slightly embarrassed look. We gave a few quiet words of thanks to the ONE who saved Walt long ago. Soon, Walt was back up on King.

Humpty Dumpty Sat on a horse
Humpty Dumpty fell with a great force
All the Kings family
And all the Kings friends
Prayed that he would get back up on him again.

The horse and rider were again reunited as one. The gentle touch and the murmurs of reassurance gave the horse immediately a quiet aura. Walt wasn't at fault for taking the vault. It is happenstance, and hands and times and forces that place us in the saddle of events. It is prayer, faith, and perseverance that keeps us there, victorious.

It was a fine day for all. Horses and men and women all took their places again and enjoyed each other as we continued to ride victoriously down the path of life.

The End

THE ROCK

W<small>E LIVED IN AN AREA</small> that once was a field where corn or beans had once grown. It was between the country and the town. My father liked to plant things. One-day while digging a hole to plant another tree he came across a small rock that protruded above the topsoil. Trying to remove it became a real task as he dug around the rock, which became larger and larger. After digging around it about a foot deep, he had a splendid idea. His two boys could earn a little extra money by extracting this hindrance for a sum that would appeal to the boys. Father came forward and proposed a dime a apiece if we would extract the rock and a quarter each if we would take it across the street yonder and deposit it where no one lived. With so much money at stake, we both jumped at the chance to earn some easy cash.

I was twelve and smart as a whip. A high intelligent forehead and an engaging smile I was at that place in my life where nothing was too difficult. A body honed to perfection by all the weed pulling, hoe wielding, and chicken house cleaning as well as a paper route

With shovels, rakes and crowbar we tackled the hard imprisoned rock with vim and vigor. We dug, heaved, and swore at the offending piece of rock. It only grew larger as we removed clay and dirt around the obstacle.

Since our being young, we began to formulate theories on how to extract the behemoth with as little real effort as possible.

"I will go and get the hose and water around the rock to loosen it up," I said with a note of victory in my young naive voice. Down at the house the hose rested where it had been since last year. Grabbing one end and trying to straighten out the fixed coiled hose, it fought back with all of its might. After a considerable time I was able to get the hose in some sort of resemblance of a straight conduit, only to find it did not reach the rock. My brother all the while was sitting on the offending object laughing at all of my endeavors. I was approaching the boiling point when I said, "its your turn to get another length of hose in the garage so we can reach the stone." My sibling was not amused but sullenly started for the garage while I sat on our adversary chuckling at our predicament. When brother finally brought up the extra length of hose I suggested when he returned to the house to turn on the water he bring up a nozzle to blast the clay away from the rock. With much mumbling and unhappiness, brother turned on the water and retrieved the nozzle. Getting the nozzle on the hose was difficult task as we both tried to bend the hose and screw on the nozzle at the same time, resulting in wetness of both clothes and body. When brother started the blasting away of the clay, a backlash of muddy water completed the wet and near defeated scene. Brother said, "I am quitting this farce and you can have both dimes when you extract this antagonist.

I also stropped and left the battlefield until tomorrow when I might think of more good ideas. The next day I sought one of my Friends for help and encouragement especially since dad was making enquires on my progress since we had spent so much time yesterday. "Since your brother has quit I imagine twenty cents is looking mighty big for such a little job," said father with a hint of amusement in his voice.

"I am going to get my friend, Packy, to help me for the fun of it," I retorted with a much bravado I could muster at the breakfast table.

Packy and I walked back to the rock for an assessment by a new mind. Packy was of a mind to get a sledgehammer and beat it to death. "Ok you get your hammer and I'll wait here and think if we need anything else for this job." Packy went on his way to fetch the ultimate of many stubborn problems.

On his return, he wanted to start the process immediately, which I hesitantly agreed. With up-raised hammer and arms, Packy began to blast the rock with many blows that would break any regular stone or rock. The only advancement he made was to splinter off piercing shads and splinters that found their way into our faces and arms. When Packy finally wearied, I took a turn only to find the rock was not giving one inch in size or its contrary nature. When both of us were lying down, panting and exhausted we thought up another way to defeat this adversary.

"Why don't we start about five feet away from the rock and build a declining ramp so we can get a crowbar or spud bar under the thing and pry it out after we reach its bottom."

Packy was the same age as me therefore we thought alike.

"Good idea. I'll get another shovel so we can both tackle this ramp."

Going back to the house, I found myself moseying along with the devious notion that Packy would have much of the ramp job done by the time I came back with the spare shovel. When I returned with the spare shovel, Packy was leaning on his shovel. Nor one spade full of dirt had been removed. We both thought alike.

'While you were gone, a long time I thought, I began to think, before we started digging we would have to decide which side the ramp should be on and if five feet was enough. We both thought a like and Packy just proved it.

Let's start on this side of the rock and begin at five feet. We can make adjustments later if need be.

Both of us began to dig from five feet out aiming at the base of Rambo the Rock. The soil and clay still was muddy so we wondered why. Checking the hose, that we had left it in the pit and found the nozzle leaking water all the while we planned the ramp attack. Packy began to shovel out dirt at the five-foot mark and I fought with muddy water and clay.

The digging took most of our day therefore; we stopped and agreed we would both start again tomorrow.

That night I had trouble getting to sleep. My hands had a few blisters and my back felt out of joint, only the quarters and the power they represented took me off to a dreamland where rocks flew at a command and boys ate candy all day long.

In the morning, my dad again asked about our progress and I was chagrined to report that we had not removed the rock nor had we come its bottom. When Packy arrived rested and full of vim and vinegar we attacked the beastie once again. When we finally reached, what we thought was the bottom we used the spud bar that Packy had brought from his Uncle Cuppie's garage. Jamming the bar under the rock, we tried every way we could think of to free the giant hard mineral deposit. Straining at the bar and jumping on it brought only pain and discouragement. As we talked about abandoning the task, old man Bumpke came over the fence from his field and walked up to our project rubbing his chin. The old man had owned our field at one time where our house now stood.

"I see you boys have your hands full trying to free that boulder from its hiding place. My grand pap and I came across this bad boy years ago when it inhabited our field. Grand pap used our old mule and a deep plow to free it from its earthly abode. He said we should 'take it over YONDER where no one lived and bury it out of sight,' which we did. Now that you are resurrecting it what you gonna do with it?'

"We haven't got it out yet. When we do my dad said to "take it across the street over YONDER where no one lives and bury it out sight."

"Well, if you boys don't mind I can get my tractor with its front loader and come over and finish the job since my Grand pap was the one that buried it there."

So that is just what old man Bumpke did for us. We buried it over yonder where no on lived. I gave Packy a dime for helping and I became for several weeks the rich boy of the neighborhood. Filling in the hole is another story.

Years later I was in the area and thought I would drive past the old place and give it a look for old times sake. Driving down the road I glance across the road and saw houses built over yonder. Someone had found the buried boulder and used it for the center of a beautiful flower garden.

The End

CHICKEN SURPRISE

A CHICKEN AND RICE GO TOGETHER real nice. How about a chicken house and cerebral exercise? That is in the story and needs to be explained because it is part of the surprise.

During the big WW II, it was sensible for folks to provide some of their own food. Most goods and foods were rationed. Coupon books were allocated for sugar, shoes, and other scarce commodities. Blue and red tokens were distributed to the populace for the right to buy beef and pork. The whole process produced a people that were thankful and resourceful concerning the consumable merchandise scarcities. Our neighbors all began to pitch in by starting and maintaining Victory Gardens. We took turns in the neighborhood driving to the grocery and then only on a weekly basis or even less often. Canning jars and water baths for processing came out from the inner recesses of basements to be put on the front lines of the war effort. One by one, the neighbors in our area began to build or rebuild chicken houses so that fresh meat and eggs would be available. Some people in town even used piano crates to make that important chicken coop. Lumber was difficult to find and therefore, much recycling was put into play. Nothing was wasted.

My father, in his desire to cooperate began to think about what we would do for the fresh meat situation. He saw an ad in the newspaper for a child's play house. After looking at it and seeing in his mind's eye that it would make a fine chicken coop he bought it. A few nights later, a big truck rolled up and began to navigate into our back yard to the spot where Dad had picked out for it to rest. It was located about 200 feet behind the house on a little rise that was the highest place on the property

The property was a little less that two acres but was already filled with practical plantings. A grape arbor and a large garden. Apple trees. Peach trees. Elderberries bushes. Raspberries. Strawberry patch. Now with the addition of chickens, it would be a cornucopia of edibles. With each new addition, I was learning that new responsibilities and efforts were only a short distance behind.

I saw the playhouse and was impressed with its quaint architectural and rustic appearance. Even so, I could see work disguised behind the facade as well as fried chicken on Sundays. It had little windows on all sides and a door that required most people to stoop before entering. The roof was pitched and covered with wooden shingles. The sides were wood slates, and everything was brown. It is hard to remember but the inside dimensions must have been about 6 feet by 6 feet. Small enough to be brought in on the bed of a dump truck. As a kid, I could stand up in the center and not feel claustrophobic. With much grunting and yelling the dump truck slowly let the little house slide down the truck bed onto the awaiting concrete blocks were it would rest for many years.

We cut a trap door behind the little playhouse and eventually bought some biddies and put them in the room. We built a chicken roost where about sixteen adult birds could winter over. On the opposite side of the tiny room we built, four egg laying nests. Each spring we would buy about 50 little chicks and raise them to pullets. In the summer and fall, we had a surplus of fryers and more eggs than we could eat. The surplus eggs we put down in a crock that had layers of salt brine, eggs, and water glass in layers. This method kept the eggs without refrigeration for many months. When mother wanted some eggs for a recipe, she sent me to the basement where I approached the vat with rolled up sleeves and pursed lips. Gently reaching into that cold, slimy mass,

I carefully searched until the requested number of unbroken eggs had been retrieved. As winter approached, we killed and dressed all the chickens that we could not winter over and canned or sold them.

The chicken house became a permanent part of the landscape on the diminutive farm we called home. It was a reference point for most of the objects and events that were in the vicinity. The fruit trees started where the chicken house was located. The grape arbor was 30 feet to the right of the chicken house. The raspberries were located on the left just a little beyond the chicken house. The compost pile was just to the left of the chicken house. The garden stopped at the chicken house. Some geese flew over just behind the chicken house. The barbecue grill was halfway between the house and the chicken house. I put up a basketball pole and hoop just to the left of the chicken house.

In the winter after a big snow, it was all I could do to make it to the chicken house. I would light my little kerosene lantern and start to trudge up the brick path that could be partly shoveled. That went as far as the start of the garden. From that point on, it was the hard ground and uncharted pathway to the far end of the garden and then the chicken house. Inside the little house, all was cozy and serene. In the middle of the room, we had a space kerosene heater turned on low that kept the birds warm. They sat on the roost and with low clucking sounds approved of my visit. I brought fresh water, mash, grit, and a little corn rounded out my gifts. I soon gathered up their gifts to us. Carefully putting the eggs in a secure carton, I soon returned to the frigid outdoors with my little lantern that bravely pierced the early morning darkness for my journey back to the house. I repeated this process for several years until dad bought some outdoor spotlights that flooded the backyard making the little lantern unnecessary. I cleaned the lantern and put it away thinking sometime later I would show my Grandchildren the object that had accompanied me on so many early morning missions, just before going to school. We soon stopped using the kerosene space heater for one reason or another and set it aside for another day. I then used the spotlights for light to find my way back up the path to the little chicken house. The War eventually, concluded and the raising of chickens did too. The expenses kept going up and the motivation kept going down until one day there was only one chicken left.

His name was Biggie. He was my pet. A giant white Plymouth Rock rooster. He came when I called his name. He strutted all around me but never attacked. When others came too close, the rooster sometime would run to them and fly up and with his immense spurs trying to attack people. He was a big, proud animal with no one left to show off to. All the others had withdrawn and had become someone's Sunday dinner. I noticed the feed barrel getting low but was not too concerned for Biggie who was able to forage for himself in the grass most of the day. The feed would last for many moons to come, I thought. One night as winter approached, I came home from my paper route, it was late. My mother met me on the porch with some coins and news. "Biggie is dead. Take this money, go back uptown, and get something to eat. We are having Biggie for supper tonight," she said. I ran from the house and left the cannibals to their culinary ritual. I hurried through the dark, angry, and heartbroken night trying to fit all the parts together. My one and only pet sacrificed on the alter of miserly authorities. Hot tears streamed down my cheeks, relieving the inner pressures. After a long and lonely walk uptown, I noticed the streetlights looking down and illuminating my surroundings again. "What did I do wrong," I thought as I looked down at the silver that had been thrust into my hand. With some doubt here and some confusion there, I was certain of only one thing. The chicken house would never be the same again, nor would I.

My first taste of real money was when we sold the eggs and the chickens and split the profit with my Father. This paid better than the paper routes I had, and even the grass cutting I did each summer. Selling fruits and vegetables door to door was about as good as cutting grass, but I was limited to summer conditions etc. The eggs came almost all year, and the meat from the chickens came all at once in the late fall. When we slaughtered the extra chickens, dressed them, and then peddled them to grocery store uptown. That meant a big pay at one time and it looked good. However, after a few years I could see that a good education might carry me further in the world than poultry. I made a promise to myself after cleaning chicken roosts and putting creosote on them and the floors that I would go to college and fight my way through the maize of academia to obtain a degree. With this declaration I soon found myself in the later part of my freshman year in Pharmacy school.

Many had told me that I could **not** get a college degree. Some from my own family that doubted that I could work, play, study, and put it together for a success story. I knew that the first year was very essential. You could get good grades now so that later you could use them to maintain your averages, as the subjects finally got more difficult. I had a friend that was from my High School class that attended college with me. Rolla and I both vowed that this first two years would be devoted to good grades. We put party times, dating, and other time-consuming activities on the back burner. Each night we would gather at one of our homes after school and after work to study. This usually meant that we began about 10 P.M. after getting off work and studied until we were too tired or giddy to continue. At Rolla's house, we studied in the kitchen at the table. After some time his Mom and Pop would say good night and go to bed. The same thing happened at my house. Coffee flowed in abundance and the cigarette smoke was thick.

One fine spring evening at my house, we both had gathered to study for final exams. It was a clear cool evening. Studying was difficult; knowing summer was around the corner. We continued to pour over our studies and drink hot coffee. In those days, we smoked, and consequently, we closed the doors to the rest of the house. The windows in the kitchen were not opened enough to allow good circulation of air, and therefore the room became hot and stuffy. We decided that a break was in order if we were to continue to try to grasp the academic potpourri that yet lay before us. We adjourned to the breezeway porch and took in the invigorating night air.

Stepping off the porch, we encouraged each other to take deep knee bends and intense breathing to revitalize our bodies and thinking processes. Having done this, we began to extol the virtues of the reviving moment and theorized on the various ways to extend or magnify the present scenario. Predictably, the discussion came to the vision of bodies unencumbered by clothes, dancing in the cool, intoxicating night air. This would positively be the ultimate in joy and release from the tight confines of the study ritual. After a few minutes of mental flights of fancy, the talk turned to bold challenges. The braggarts threw about specifics and particulars until one of us picked up the gauntlet. "I'll do it for a dollar." I heard myself say.

What we had decided upon was that I would shed all my clothes and in the buff run to the chicken house, around it, and return in the soft, black, spring night. At 1:30 A.M., even the lights from the far off town would give me little help in finding my way in the pitch dark. I was confident that having traveled that course a thousand times that I wouldn't fall or even stub my toes. The dollar would be a big help also. It would buy three box lunches at the School or buy 3 or 4 gallons of gas for my green monster of a car. I was only making about 50 to 60 cents an hour at the drug store so I had surely made one sweet wager that spelled quick profits and little effort. I played sports and ran track. This whole event should last less than one minute and have lasting overtones of victory and boldness to my lifelong friend. I could do this!

I moved to the corner of the garage and began to peel off my clothes in a neat little pile. Socks and shoes had to go because that was the final condition of the wager. Everything stacked neatly for a quick retrieval upon my speedy return. I made a quick and automatic scan of all that was about me, keeping Rolla at my back to preserve my dignity. I took a deep breath and made the initial lunge in the direction of the chicken house. Springing into the soft, inky night was a little scary at first.

I had made many wagers before. We would bet on bowling or even a pool game. I bet once on the result of swimming a flood stage river. Bike races, push ups, even scores on tests. It seemed that these wagers were not to make money but to improve ones skills and abilities. It also was a way to feel superior occasionally in a world that naturally compressed the meek and faltering into the background of life. I probably lost as many wagers as I had won. The wagers were never large. The winning was well worth the sting of defeats. A fellow could live a long time in a victory. I had learned to put defeats in boxes and victories under magnifying glasses. This victory tonight would be very valuable in the years to come; I thought as I picked up momentum.

A few feet from the chicken house was a tiny wooden bridge that I leaped across to avoid splinters and to pick up speed. I looked ahead but could not see the chicken house yet because of the blanket of darkness. It was as though I were rushing into a black velvet fog. Out of my peripheral vision, I saw the great Maple tree I planted years ago to my right. To the left was the faint outline of other fauna and overhanging branches that verified I was heading in the correct direction. Under my feet was the hard remnant of the old brick path that was laid down years before by my own hands. That gave me the assurance that even in the dark I was in contact with familiar things. Soon, I left the brick area and now enjoyed the cushion effect that the spring earth gave the barefoot boy. The barely discernible outline of the very familiar chicken house came into my sights, up ahead. To the right of me the new garden gave off its unique earthy aroma. To the left was the old concrete block barbecue grill that had helped to host many picnics. I was on the right track. Quickly the chicken house loomed before me in all its cuteness and memories. I must slow a little as I turn and go around the little house insuring that a slip would not be in my repertoire. Behind the former poultry domicile the night was even more enveloping. There, a special spot of frigid air ran over my dedicated body, as for the first time I remembered my nakedness and vulnerability to things that go thump in the night. Here was the old orchard now complete with overgrown bushes and grasses that prospered in the area where at one time the chickens were confined. The posts and fences having deteriorated, but it was still an area of particular high nutrient value for fauna. Another deep breath as I rounded the diminutive building and headed back down the path to home and clothes. In the scene before me at this early morning hour was auspicious. The neighbor's houses were barley visible and dark as tombs. Our house presented a gray outline with no lights observable except the faint outline of the upstairs bathroom window where we always had a night-light. My arms at my sides pumping forward and back like pistons. My legs moving high and in cadence with the tempo of the rest of my body. The whole of the fluid-like movements began to be like a dreamy existence. Everything began to take on a slow motion affect as the heady taste of victory and financial reward began to infuse itself in my physical being. More than halfway back to my house the high springy steps of the race seemed to last for minutes. In the graceful movements, I drank in the narcotic stuff of inner fulfillment. This race is mine. This story is mine. That dollar is mine. I beat the challenge and quenched the dare.

On my many stag-like leaps, I kept a subconscious scanning of my position. The house was closer, the path beneath me would soon turn into old bricks, and a slow down would have to be effected for a safe landing. On one of my bounding vaults, in mid air, I perceived a flickering flash and just as sudden an explosion of light from two directions. They appeared to me to be the angry eyes of divine origin from the heights of heaven. I had done something slightly unclean and now in mid flight I was discovered naked and illuminated for all of the heavenly host to cluck disapproval and disgust. As I came back to the earth's surface and reevaluated my circumstances I determined that it was my friend Rolla who had turned on the outside flood lights that Dad had installed to dispel the early morning darkness for chicken keepers. With this new information in my stunned brain, I was able to make the last few yards of the journey with some type of hand covering maneuvers. My face red with rage at the friend I had trusted, I hurriedly put on my clothes. Mutterings filled with anger and oaths at my questionable friend were soon turned back to confident words of achievement. The lights turned off, the dollar in hand, and the thought that no one knows-all made for a speedy recovery to normality. We decided that we had studied enough, and it would be sensible to call it a day or night. And we did.

This secret stayed sealed for over **thirty** years. At a family gathering, it seemed that the subject turned to events such as this and how it was safe now to divulge them to those that love you. I carefully told the story to my family and all were engrossed in its content. Looking for weaknesses in leaders and saints was once my role as a younger listener. After this story was told, there were a few laughs and guffaws. My sister seemed to have an all knowing look on her face as she began to recount that very night from her perspective. She told of hearing low muffled voices one night just below her window behind the house. The voice was intense she said, and then they fell quietly. She thought she saw movement in the back yard going to the chicken house. Straining her eyes for a better view all appeared dark and still. All of a sudden the view before her turned into a stage-like brilliance that left no detail in doubt. The lights were on and reveled her most esteemed brother running down the old chicken house path with nothing on but a surprised look. Blinking to see whether that was what was really in her back yard, the surprise was over and disappeared into the protection of the house. Silent all these years, she had kept the secret to herself. That's what good sisters do.

I often think of that night when I hear of dares and wagers. It didn't hurt anyone. It wasn't vulgar or destructive. It was fun for Rolla my friend. It was a surprise to Jane, my sister. For me, the chicken keeper turned the night into a surprised

Leaper becoming a dollar reaper.

The End

THE PAPER ROUTE

MY FIRST REAL PAYING JOB was when I was twelve years old, was a paper route. It was 1945, and my resources were at a low ebb. My meagerly week's allowance was just not enough to sustain a young boy with grand needs and ideas. I was attaining an age when a boy wanted more than ten cents a week with no chance of improvement. The news about an open paper route came to my attention via a friend who knew a friend that had been on the route. I made the necessary phone call to the powers in charge and was told someone would meet me after school on Friday with all the particulars. This meeting took place punctually at the place specified

A middle-aged man met me, and we had our meeting at Sam's hamburger joint. Free coffee and a burger was a good beginning. The man introduced himself as a regional manager of the SHOPPING NEWS. A paper that came out on Thursdays of each week that contained all kinds of advertisements and coupons for the downtown Cincinnati merchants. He had arranged for the papers to be delivered to the porch on an agreeing person living on the route itself. I would go to that address and tote the papers on the route that I would soon see. A map of the route and the number of papers would be provided when I gathered the papers on Thursday. After coffee he made some more enquiries and asking about any previous work experience I might have had. Most of the talking was finished. He gave me a map of the porch drop-off, and it was covered with little notations as well as rules and regulations of the Shoppers News required of paperboys must adhere to. He made it crystal clear if those rules were not adhered to I would be dismissed. With these grand and ponderous instructions, he asked me whether I had any questions.

Naturally, I asked about the pay. He told me, a check would arrive in the mail, usually on Fridays and I could cash it at the bank. The rate was ninety cents a week with no benefits. I was happy but not thrilled as he gave me his card and stated that if for any reason I needed to talk to him about the route to give him call.

I could hardly wait until next Thursday rolled around. Meanwhile, I rode my bike to the address he had given me for the paper drop. The house was very common for those days with a big porch covered and partly enclosed by high sides made of brick. (A good place in case of rain or snow.)

I told some of my friends I would soon be rolling in dough with my new job. My other jobs were mostly selling fruit, and vegetables door to door when we had a surplus in our garden or when Dad bought stuff at farmer's market at the Cincinnati Farmers Market. We also sold chickens and eggs if we could spare them. This provided me with a good source of funds in the summer but left me flat broke the rest of the year.

Thursday rolled around and after school I made haste to begin my new Work life. I was certain that this good event would propel me into the stratosphere of the rich and famous. Arriving at the porch I was shocked to find more papers that could be delivered all week. My heart fell to the ground as I mentally tried to figure how many papers they had left. A nice touch was the new and bright canvas paper bag, highly starched and emblazoned with the *Shoppers News* Logo.

As I was grumbling around looking at my map and wondering how in the world I could deliver all these papers before sun down Saturday. Just then another boy came up on the porch and addressed me as the new boy. He was the old boy, and half of those papers were his. He also informed me that the best way to distribute the massive number of issues was to take half the papers and do half the route returning here for the other half and the finish up here and get home before dark.

It was a good plan and with some clumsiness I could follow the old boy's suggestion and got home just at dark. I was tired and ached because of all that weight on my skinny shoulder. Nothing when compared to on the next day.

The check did not arrive as related to me by my regional manager. The next day Friday) I was thinking of quitting this worthless job when my mother said I had a letter in the mail. (Saturday) With anticipation running high, I opened the letter to find a check for ninety cents with my name on the front. It also contained a note explaining the slight delay in delivery.

"Since you are a new employee of Shopping News, the book work concerning your information took an extra day to post. Sorry for any inconvenience. In the future the check should arrive punctually on Fridays."

The route gave me a sense of responsibility even in the winter when the snow was six inches deep and zero degrees outside. Contrary to popular belief I received very few tips at Christmas time. I did get some hot chocolate on occasion as the temperature dipped near zero. Week after week the papers were delivered, through rain and snow and sleet. Hot sun, windy days, and humid days the paper must go through. Feet hurt? Tough stuff. Legs and back distributing signs of pain and over use! Who cares? Wear it out with more walking was the advice I received from those who where supposed to love me. Hard work was the path to acceptance and righteousness.

The checks were the same whether hot or cold days. It made no difference. These checks came right on time for the next year or so. One day I had a phone call from my employer asking whether I would interested in a new position with The News as a route monitor. I replied by asking about the duties and pay. He replied that a route monitor paid one dollar and twenty-five cents as well as any reimbursement of any travel expenses. (On my up?) I answered in the affirmative and was given the details on my duties. I would be given two maps each week by mail. I would go to that destination and by using the map and good sense I would follow that Shopper News paperboy to report on his delivery. We were not allowed to cross any lawns. Each paper had to be folded in a manner so that when placed tightly between the door and its jam it would fall and open up as the homeowner opened his door. No dumping of papers in sewers or creeks or gullies. All of these rules I had obeyed during my time as delivery boy so it must have seemed that I was a good and conscience boy to be a route monitor. I had to travel throughout Hamilton County and Cincinnati to monitor different routes and boys. Even in some of the toughest parts of town I executed my job flawlessly.

One of the best perks to this job was that I could travel to my destinations and tabulate the cost per bus or trolley and then submit that amount each week with my reports to submit for reimbursement. This procedure gave me an opportunity to thumb around town and to meet people. It was very lucrative. The dimes and quarters would pile up and be added to my weekly check. These coins I could save by thumbing around the county, and the report the cost that buses and trolleys would have cost me had I used them. (Illegal?) I never questioned it because other monitors did the same. My first taste of business ethics.)

I would call in each Thursday eve and give my report and expenses over the phone. I was never questioned about any expense so they must have thought it was a deal for them too.

Thumbing around all over the area gave me a sense of adventure as well as education. I met folks from all walks of life and would occasionally help them.

One time a man was selling bibles and talked my arm off and then admitted his heart was not into his job. Letting me out of the car he said, "The Bible is perfect but those that handle them are not."

One time a lady couldn't see very well and had me tell her when a traffic light appeared or a stop sign. She stopped at her house finally as she wanted me to help unload her purchases, which I did. She then told me, my destination was down the street, about five blocks.

This job was the first of many and taught me much about myself and others. The difficulties never hurt me; in fact, they gave me the ability to do things others only talk about. A sense of adventure will be a lasting advantage to those who try it.

The End

FIFI AND BLONDIE

Y OU MEET SUCH INTERESTING PEOPLE when you
work in a drug store. When you own the store you
not only meet them, but you also get to really know them.
Such was the case of Fifi. In my store in Logan, Ohio, we were
always busy—especially at the lunch counter where a group
of regulars kept us entertained and amused.

One person that comes to mind was a retired, one-armed
baseball player. One day while he was drinking his coffee,
he demanded I give him a knife. Since he was only drinking
coffee, I couldn't figure out why he needed one and told him
so. After much cursing and several loud oaths from him, I
finally relented and gave him one. He took the knife by the
blade end in his one good hand, stood up, and with a great
round-house swing, came down on that poor, lonely, half-
full coffee cup and broke it into a thousand pieces. He then
declared to everyone at the lunch counter that no longer
would that "CRACKED cup be used to serve coffee to poor
innocent patrons at this establishment."

Then there was Old Man Miller. He liked to hunt and
fish and go mushroom hunting. Since he lived alone, he
would bring in his catch and have my cook prepare it for
him. The condition was that any excesses go to the cook and
the storeowner. Sometimes we would wait until the store
closed and then get out the goodies to cook and eat. I can
still taste some of the great morel mushrooms, soaked in
saltwater first to force out all the little bugs from the sponge-
like crevices. Then we cut the mushrooms down the center
and then fried them on both sides in real creamery butter.
There was nothing like that heavenly aroma. Put 2 or 3 of

those morels on some buttered home-baked bread and you are in pig heaven.

Then there was Fifi. A sizable woman with a sizable need to influence the lives of people around her, Fifi had a lot of time on her hands and spent a lot of it at our lunch counter. All her children had married and left the nest. Her husband was a successful businessman and consequently spent much of his time away from the home. At first, when she came in for lunch, she just ate slowly, spending a couple hours visiting, nibbling, reading, conversing, etc. The span of her activities began to increase as she began to clear the tables, give suggestions to patrons, and generally make herself at home. Fifi continued to enlarge her sphere of influence, until it began to consume everyone nearby.

One evening after a long, hard pharmacy day, I heard a great commotion coming from the lunch counter area. It sounded like two wildcats and a porcupine locked in mortal combat in a gunnysack. I dropped all my life-and-death activities at the Pharmacy area and ran over to the soda fountain. To my surprise there—on the floor of my friendly, quiet, corner, neighborhood, rural drug store—wrestled two people of the female persuasion.

One of them wore a uniform and had mostly blond hair (except at the roots, where much black and some red was showing). The other person was large and wore what at one time had been an expensive and classy black dress with gold trim and rhinestone buttons (some were still left). I jumped into the middle of that struggle when I recognized them as Fifi and one of my waitresses. (I'll call her Blondie.)

I remembered that elective course from Pharmacy School, Fisticuffs 101, and remembered how important the first few moments of discord can be. The book said a mediator should take a firm hand to the situation and pry loose the death grips using soothing counseling terms such as, "Stop this fighting or I'll kill you both and call the cops!" Therefore, I did.

The up righting of bodies, the straightening of clothes, the repositioning of hair, and the smoothing of feathers began. Each she-wrestler returned to her corner as I began to make inquiries. Hankies and oaths were the order of the day, as Fifi told of over-hearing Blondie calling her overweight (using a phrase indicating Fifi's resemblance to an unruly elephant. At that time, Fifi was out of sight, maybe bending over the dish washing machine, but not out of hearing range, when Blondie admitted the indiscretion and also impressed upon me its factual basis. Then they both went home. Fifi in a huff and Blondie to cool off. Therefore, did I eventually, go home to rest; home sweet home; rest, and sweet quiet?

But the phone rang, at 3 am! It was Fifi. She wanted me to fire Blondie. She couldn't sleep; the brawl made her nervous. She might talk to her lawyer. Will I fire her? "No," I said. She hung up.

Next day, no Fifi. Peace and quiet. Next night: Another phone call at 3 a.m.: "It's me, Mr. Pansing; Fifi. I can't sleep. You must fire Blondie. It's only right. I'm still nervous. You have lost a good customer in me. My lawyer will be back in town tomorrow." Click.

A few more late night calls and then nothing. Not threatening but slightly acidic. Well, we didn't see Fifi for several weeks. Occasionally I would see her in town and wave and say hi. No response. Once we met in the bank and I said she should come see us. Ice cold silence. After a few months and some prayer, the Lord suggested I send some sort of gift to mend the fences. I sent her some roses and a note of reconciliation. Little by little, Fifi came back and became a cautious customer, buying newspapers, candy, and a few odds and ends. Eventually a lunch or snack was her only gesture of reconciliation but always when Blondie was not on duty.

It was never quite the same, even though we exchanged pleasantries and smiles. Fifi did teach me a very important lesson. The customer may not always be right, but she is always the customer.

The End

MOUNTAIN JUSTICE

F OR YEARS, THE MONTH OF November meant more
than snow flurries, roast turkey and pumpkin pie.
It meant buying special clothing, and equipment. It meant
the preparation for the privileged few that would soon be
heading up into the mountains of West Virginia for our
annual Deer Hunt. The three days before Thanksgiving was
the beginning of high power rifle deer season. Time to think
about thick socks, warm cap, thermal underwear, lined
gloves and other outdoors clothing. Equipment was checked
and evaluated. Remembering last years outing one would
buy thicker socks or gloves if warranted. I was cleaning my
rifles and buying shells that were part of the ritual. My duffel
bag was set out many days in advance of my departure so
that all the needed paraphernalia would find its way in that
sack. I knew that on the mountain I could only rely on what
I had brought. Few stores in my area would have the special
stuff big game hunters required.

Finally, the big day arrived. The Saturday before the
Monday of the first day. I was up early and packed the car
with everything I needed for this excursion. For days, I had
watched the weather reports. Snow in the mountains was
desirable. This helped in tracking the deer and gave the day
a brighter and longer presentation. There was no snow on
the ground here in Ohio but the weather maps showed that
up in the Appalachian Mountains the snow was present and
sufficient. The weather maps indicated a small storm in the
western part of the country would head our way next week.
All in all, it appeared to be a good weather forecast for the
hunting expedition.

I left my little world behind as the car began to wind through the foothills of West Virginia and eventually on to Good Hope, W. Va. My wife had called this little town home for years. Her uncle Darrell still lived here. I was to meet with him there and then transfer all my hunting possessions to his little Scout 4 wheel drive vehicle.

I arrived on time and was treated to the usual gracious hospitality of my in-laws. Mugs of hot coffee and mounds of mashed potatoes. Pan-fried meat and savory green beans. Cakes and pies that were of award winning quality and visual masterpieces. Never ending talk of the weather, hunting conditions and hunts gone by. Up dated reports on the hunting companions that had preceded us up the mountains. Stocking up and packing away the culinary offerings from Aunt Dorothy. Pepperoni rolls, vegetable soup, cookies, and other delectable foods. Finally, all is packed in the little sure footed 4 wheel drive Scout, for the long, winding trip up the mountains to Canaan valley and our cabin. A few miles out of town, we picked up some more of our party. Bob and Bill were ready and waiting in their red Jeep. Now on to the hunt.

The little caravan made good time on the roads. Up one hill and down another. Each time gaining some altitude until we noticed a thin white covering of snow on the ground. The air began to get colder as the sun was now going down quickly behind the impending Appalachian Mountains in the distance. The dark world of night soon enveloped the hopeful hunters and their spirited transportation. Chugging along at a predictable rate, the motorized porters belied their age and demanding tenure of service. Sometimes purring like a kitten, sometimes growling like a lion they kept taking us higher and higher into the regions of elevated altitude. Now they left tracks in the newly fallen snow. With snow now on the road and temperatures dropping, the rear end of one and then the other vehicles would fishtail. After several of these episodes, the lead vehicle occupants would begin honking their horn, waving hands and blinking lights, as it pulled over to the next wide place in the highway. We followed right behind. All the men piled out and began to zip up and button up as the mountain wind and chill cut through the night. Hats pulled down and gloves went on as the conditions were discussed and evaluated. It was time to turn in the hubs on the front wheels so that the advantage of four-wheel drive would be available. Each driver, knelt in the snow by the axle hub of each front wheel and with someone holding a flashlight began the arduous task of turning the hub nut to engage the four-wheel drive feature. The process required some grunts and groans and even on oath or two. Ultimately, all the front wheels of both of our chariots were now engaged and we were ready to assume our trek up the mountain.

Retreating into the enclosed coziness of the four wheelers we soon began to see road signs that indicated we were close to our destination. Only one more mountain to climb. The snow had stopped but the road was still very slippery. We began to lose traction and some of us would jump out and push the vehicles until we again gained some momentum. This exercise was not only a wonderful way to keep warm but also let us work off some old flatland's fat we had brought along. As we neared the top of this mountain, we were thankful we had previously agreed to stop at the little country store on the edge of the Canaan State Park to pick up a few supplies we had neglected to get. Pulling over in front of the little back woods store, we sighed a sigh of relief that we were almost to our cabin.

Inside the store, we could loosen our clothing a little more and relax for a time. Several other men were in the store talking to the owner about the opening day of deer season. We listened intently to see if any news might apply to us. It wasn't long before our boys were in the conversation, asking about conditions, such as weather on top of Cabin Mountain and deer herd size. We all chimed in about last year's hunt and what was happening to the valley. We were told about fire permits that were now required and written permission to hunt in certain places. The price of licenses was going up and that more snow was predicted. We selected our purchases and paid for them. With a few parting words of "see you later", and "have a good hunt", the little band of like-minded men dispersed, never to gather quite in the same form or fashion again. We hit the mountain's serving of wind and cold and scrambled into the little iron transportation to continue to the cabin.

Just a few more miles and the entrance to the state park was visible and welcome. We turned in and slowly wound our way up the long driveway. Our eyes were glued to the parks meadows. The headlights were weaving and bobbing across the landscape. Summarily, by chance they fell upon shiny, almost glowing receivers that indicted deer eyes. We would stop and turn down the windows to spot the inquisitive four-footed animal with our binoculars. Each of us would estimate the size and sex of the creature and then we would slowly go on, hoping for more sightings. This occurred every night when we returned from hunting all day. It was good practice, we thought, as we slowly came into the area that the cabin was located. With the cabin's number on our lips, we slowly drove around the loop that they were located in the park. We found it with lights on to welcome us home. A honk of the horns and we were soon greeted by those that had arrived earlier. Hearty hello's and pats on the back. "How have you been?" "Looks like you have put on weight." "Lost some hair, I see." Comments passed all around and no one was spared the spotlight for a moment or two. Rooms and beds were selected and gear stowed away so that the fun could begin. I could smell that someone was cooking supper. The warmth of the place suggested that a fire in the fireplace had been roaring earlier. Almost every corner of each bedroom had nestled in them a gun or gun case. Giant coats, boots of all description, gloves, and binoculars, hats of many shapes, were scattered about everywhere. I was back home in the nest of stalwart hunter's togetherness.

We ate well. We slept well. On Sunday, we rested and walked around the park to check out the other hunters. We strolled down to the Park Lodge to check out the restaurant and other facilities. We then drove around the golf course and checked the snow for deer tracks. We saw a few deer on the edge of the woods and then came back to the cabin for a pleasant evening and preparations for tomorrow. One or all prepared our evening meal. A good meal was boiled potatoes, carrots, and onions. All topped off with corned beef. This would be followed by some cake or pie. One of our group was a fireman that had chef's duty at home that prepared him for scrumptious meals for the hunters.

Then off to the great room where the fire had been built back up and was now glowing with warmth and hospitality. Long discussions of politics, hunting techniques, morals and work situations, were the norm for these evenings. The time quickly moved on. We must now prepare for the next morning. Make sandwiches and pack boxes with provisions for the whole of the next day. Off to bed.

Up at 5 A.M. and make breakfast. Pancakes, eggs, and bacon were the standards to get off on the right start. Hot coffee made and poured into thermos bottles for the all day adventure. The drivers went out and cleaned off the vehicles from a small accumulation of snow. They would then start up the engines to get them and the interiors warm for the long trek up Cabin Mountain. All was ready. With some last words of inquiry we started. "You have the keys to the cabin?" "Everybody have plenty of shells?" "Don't forget your binoculars." "Did you pack the food?" (one year we forgot he food.) And on it went as we loaded up all the equipment and ourselves. We felt our pockets to make sure each and every little comfort that we required could be found. Tums for the tummy? Off we went.

Down the Park drive way and out on the road to the little schoolhouse. Turn off and start up the mountain. With each progressing moment, we could tell that the mountain got snowed on last night. Up and up and around the narrow turns and bends we went. It was still pitch dark as we turned in our seats to look back down the road towards the valley below. Little lights twinkled around the barns and houses of the rapidly diminishing farms and homesteads of Canaan Valley. Up ahead the road began to give signs of few if any recent travelers. Finally, we entered the National forest and came upon the first gap where campers and hunters were just beginning to stir after last night's mountain snowfall. We continued through the camper's gap and labored by grimacing inside and by pushing outside, the mule-like, little four wheeled vehicles onward and upward. On top of the mountain the wind had swept it almost clear. The wind blew constantly. The few trees on the top had branches on only one side of its trunk because of it. We now needed to dip down off the top to get the area we always liked to hunt. The snowdrifts became too deep and the trail too difficult to continue. The mountain has a mind and weather of its own. It said stop and we did.

We took some positions in the area and waited for the sun to come up. Finding the perfect spot was difficult and laborious in the dark. The sun finally came up and we could see that the area had been hard hit with snow even plastered on the sides of trees. Most of the morning, we fought the deep snow and could tell that the deer were not moving. It was agreed that we would return to lower levels and try not to fight the mountain any longer. We returned to surroundings that are more amicable and finally back to the cabin.

We went up the road to the Old Stone Motel where we had stayed other years to see if anyone, we knew might be in the vicinity. We decided to eat at the old restaurant. After eating, a Natural Resources Officer had alerted the people in the restaurant that two people were lost in the woods and soon they were forming a search party to go look for them. All those that wanted to volunteer to help, please meet outside in 30 minutes. We all wanted to help and formed with the group a half hour later. We were told how we would search. We broke up into groups by the Officers and sent into the woods to search. About 25 men had gathered and the officers began to teach the process of using signals and how long to search. We were looking for a man and his son that had been missing for about twelve hours. More snow and bitter cold weather was forecast for the night. We were ready and willing to exert this kind of effort for a fellow hunter, when someone came and told the two Dept. of Natural Resources Officers that the two hunters had come out of the woods this morning and were all right. We were all relieved and summarily dismissed by the two Officers with thanks and appreciation. We returned to the cabin in a gentle snow from the North. We related all the possible horrors of being lost in the mountains overnight and concluded with utterances of thanksgiving. We nestled-in, back at the cabin and retired with the glow of the knowledge we had offered ourselves to help our fellow man.

In the morning, we could see that it had snowed more during the night. The radio told of the great snowfall in the region and cautioned everyone not to travel unnecessarily. We agreed not to climb the mountain today, but with the 4 wheelers, we would seek out some new hunting territory. We loaded up the vehicles and took off for the nearby town and then out the iron bridge to the big valley flats. Finding a place that was secluded, we proceeded to move out into the snow-covered area looking for deer signs. The snow was deep and we split up to search for tracks to see if the area was worthy of our presence. I climbed up to a little ridge that overlooked a small valley that suggested a great place for deer to congregate when the weather was unforgiving, like this day. Not being able to see as far into the valley as desired, I stepped onto a huge boulder that protruded up from the valley floor up to the ridge that I had been standing on. It was covered with snow that I estimated to about two feet deep. After positioning myself on the boulder, I turned around to look back down into the little valley. Still wanting a better view, I took a step on the big rock towards its center. Suddenly the space beneath me, gave way. Its secret had been revealed by 165 pounds. I had stepped on a snow bridge that had belied the fact that the great boulder was actually two boulders divided by a small space between them. It was through this void I found myself falling. It was only an instant but I could tell that something hit me under the chin causing stars to appear. My chest received a blow from an outcropping of one of the great boulders. All of this jostling from my surroundings left me at the bottom of a stony crevice, dazed and stunned. I lay still for a moment, looking up through the new opening at the sky. No sense getting up until I felt more mentally organized, I thought. I slowly got up with great difficultly but I discovered or felt no blood on my face or head. My gloved hand still held my rifle at the ready. It looked like my newfound prison was about seven feet below the top. The boulders far ends were up against the ridge. The opposite ends pinched together like a vise.

My survival instinct told me to yell and I did. The soft snow all around and at the top seemed to muffle my attempt. I yelled again and heard no reply. What was I going to do? No one knew where I was. I was off the beaten track. The sides of the boulders were smooth and slick. No foot holds. Just when I figured that the only way out was to use heroic efforts of monumental proportions, someone called my name. I gave out a shout of relief and in just a short time my uncle Darrell was at the top of the crevice with instructions to hang on. I was given a pull up with down stretched arms. I was soon on top again, where the air was clean and the view of freedom magnificent. He told me he just happened to look in my direction from a distance when I just disappeared from sight. He thought I might be in trouble and came over to help. The yell for help facilitated his location of me. All was well and we soon left that area for lunch.

After lunch it was determined that if we went to a strip job on the other side of the town of Davis, that would enable us a better chance for finding deer. We all piled into the 4 wheelers and headed out of town and down some fire roads to the strip mine. At this point, we were at a place that we could see for a long way. A good place to scope for deer. All of us got out of the vehicles and discussed where we would hunt and headed off in several directions. I walked down the little fire road on the strip job and finally entered some wooded area. I noted that we had parked about half way down this road on private coal company property. This would give me a bearing for my return trip later this afternoon.

It didn't take too many hours of trudging through the snow covered mountain side to determine that few signs of deer were to be seen. They were hiding and would not move unless someone came upon them like rabbits and kicked them out. When this truth finally sunk into my brain, I returned to the vehicles to find that all the others had come to the same conclusion. I placed my carbine against the fender of the Scout in a stand-up position and moved into the cab for that much sought after cup of hot coffee. Bill put his gun on the hood of the Jeep and was in the cab pouring coffee. Bob was in the backseat of the Jeep with his gun enjoying coffee and a sandwich. We were telling each other what we had seen and not seen.

Suddenly without warning a roar was heard behind us as a green car approached at a high rate of speed. The auto came to a gravel-wrenching stop beside us all. Two men jumped out of that car and began to scream orders.

"Get out of the car! Don't touch anything! Step in the middle of the road and keep your hands at yours sides!" Came the instructions in almost falsetto cadence. In bewilderment, we all complied as we recognized that they were officers of the State. One of the Natural Resources Officers asked who belonged to the gun in the cab. Bob responded in the affirmative. The other officer demanded who owned the gun on the hood of the vehicle. Bill came forward and admitted ownership. The first officer came around the Scout and saw my gun laying flat on the ground in the snow. "Who's gun is this," he asked. I told him it was mine. He told me that they had been watching us with binoculars from a high vantage point and knew this rifle had been setting against the vehicle, which is illegal. "Since it was not leaning on the vehicle when we confronted you, we will not be taking you in. The other guns were in prohibited places so we will take the other two men in," he said. Bob and Bill unloaded and cased their guns. The weapons were put in the officer's car's trunk and they were taken off to visit the local Justice of the Peace.

We were stunned. It all happened so quickly. We were off the designated roadways and on private land, we thought. It was best for all of us to return to the cabin and wait for word from the two hapless hunters.

We returned to our quarters and prepared supper. The talk was centered about what would happen to Bob and Bill. Soon our wait and anxiousness was rewarded as the two hunters returned to the bosom of their comrades. Their account of the last few hours kept us hanging on each and every word. "They took us into town and made us stand before the local Justice of the Peace. He sat behind a huge desk and leered at us with one eye open and the other eye squinting to size up the situation," said Bob. He went on to describe the scene. He related that the J.P.'s great handle bar mustache twitched with anticipation as he purposefully leaned back in his chair and placed his booted feet on the cluttered desk. The old lawman began a tirade that hinted at his intention to confiscate the guns, vehicle, and impose a large fine and put the two hunters in jail. At this point Bill noticed that the two Natural Resource Officers were interjecting the circumstances that led up to the seizure of persons and equipment. At this point Bob and Bill remembered that these two officers are the men that had formed the search party the night before. They quickly reminded the officers that they had been there and offered to help. The officers remembered them and admitted to the J.P. the good citizen response of the hunters before him. Soon the railing of the wiry old West Virginia mountain man was tempered to scolding. Finally, he said, "let's just make it a hundred dollar fine. Keep your guns and Jeep." He then squeezed his forehead with his leathery hand and rolled his eyes upward. **"That's mountain justice,"** he said as he straightened up and began to turn towards a refrigerator behind him. "Want a beer," he said to the two emotionally drained defendants. Bob and Bill told him no and wanted to return to their friends.

We spent most of the evening rehashing what had happened. Most of us ultimately concluded that mountain justice was not in the mountain but in the man who looked over our shoulders. After all, it is not always justice we want but many times it is mercy. We never forgot that day, even after many more years of hunting deer on the mountain. Ultimately, we ended the week with a kink in our necks from constantly glancing behind us.

The End

TIP TOP TREK

"THOSE ARE THE MOUNTAINS IN the distance," my father said to me as we rolled along the highway in 1938. The new Ford was humming along with its nose pointing south. All eight cylinders were in harmony, producing their eighty-five-horse power for the benefit of my family on our way to Florida. My father was referring to the Smoky Mountains, many miles yet in the distance. I stood on my tiptoes in the back of the green sedan and strained to see the majesty of these famous formations. I could tell they were big. We drove for a long time and they didn't seem to get any closer. I continued to gaze and to quiz my father about the mountains until I finally gave up and lay back down to nap for a while. "Don't worry," Dad said. "Tomorrow we will be in the Smokys." And we were.

It seemed rather disappointing. We spent hours traveling in the Appalachian foothills. Signs along the road were telling us mountain this and mountain that. I couldn't tell that we were going up. We drove through Gatlinburg in the mountains. It didn't seem like we were up very high. Then we started up the road and around the curves. Even this road didn't appear to be going up all the time. The car did seem to labor more than when we were on the straight a ways yesterday. We did see some bears and even several cars that had burned up. They forgot to take out the alcohol that was used for antifreeze. We saw some cars still burning with the sad folks beside the road with their luggage held tightly in their hands. They looked so forlorn and unhappy because they didn't make it to the top. Dad had planned better, taking out the alcohol before the trip. We still noticed the Ford getting hot as it moved up the road with its cargo of four passengers and enough luggage to last us for weeks. Then, we would pull over on the berm when Dad spotted a mountain stream. My brother and I would traipse down the steep embankment with a container to retrieve the icy cold water. We returned carefully to our awaiting father who poured the precious liquid into the radiator of the thirsty Ford. This was usually repeated several times until the parched auto was satisfied. We all returned to our appointed places in the car and resumed our climb up the mountain. Little by little, I was feeling the sensation of height as more and more vistas were revealed to our upward, mobile family. Suddenly we were at the top. It was breath taking. In all directions, the views seemed to be downward. Dad parked the car and we all climbed out for a better vantage point. The Newfound Gap was the high point for us on our trip south. The air was crisp and invigorating. I ran from boulder to rock ledge for better views. I could see for miles. I thought about how many millions of people were lower than me. The scenario mesmerized me and it never has left me. We all went on to Florida but I never quite left that high place where things are different. In the years since then, I have traveled to those mountains with friends and family. We have climbed Mt. LeConte and Clingmans Dome. Cade's Cove and the Chimneys have been my destination many times. Newfound Gap and the Appalachian Trail have felt my feet in the quest for an attitude as well as altitude.

Eventually I went west and discovered for myself the Rockies and all the new scenery it represented. My eyes turned up and my heart sang at all the possibilities these new peaks and mounts conjured up. My wife and children traveled with me up and down the Rockies on the highways and byways. Something was missing. Even traveling the high Ridge Highway over the top of the Rocky Mountain National Park was not satisfying enough for the Mountain Man in me. I wanted to go because they were there. I needed a plan to get to the top of one of these babies and feel all the emotions that I remembered as a kid. I would accomplish it or know the reason why.

In 1972, my wife and our three children and I traveled through out the West on an extended vacation. The summer moved on and included many States and sights. From the west coast, we began our return journey to Ohio and the routine of every day life. We entered the State of Colorado from the west and made our first campsite in the Rockies around Grand Lake. After several days, we packed up and headed up the Ridge Road to Estes Park.

At the highest elevation of this road was a little gift shop and tourist rest area. We walked in the alpine meadows and romped on a snowfield. With great numbers of other tourists doing similar undisciplined activities, we thought we were safe from the Park Rangers and their chastisement. Wrong! We were all angrily told to get back to the tourist area and keep away from the dangers of the pristine scene but dangerous snowfield with crevices and crevasses not seen or marked. We did move back quickly. It was there that I determined to climb the highest mountain in those parts and to enjoy the unspoiled splendor of nature's alpine offering. No tourists. No congestion. No over zealous authoritarian figures.

On the eastern side of the Rockies, we camped close to the town of Estes Park. My eldest son, Mark, and I went into town and found a shop that specialized in mountain climbing. Since I thought that the training and exercise would benefit both of us in the actual climb, I hired a man who spent his summers here, teaching mountain climbing, and his winters as a ski instructor in Switzerland.

The next day we showed up for the climb. He had picked out two easy climbs, called The Twin Owls. He drove us to the location and proceeded to explain the equipment and terminology. Soon Mark and I were in the world of carabineers, braided sheath rope, brake bars, pitons, picks, and seat harnesses. With no special equipment or shoes, we began the rock ascent. The instructor went first and found a way, leaving pitons and carabineers along the way. When he found a secure place he would call out, "on belay, climb!" We would answer, "climbing." This was done as a discipline as well as the fact we couldn't always see each other for hand signals etc. Mark went second and I brought up the rear, removing the hardware from the face of the rock and putting them in a bag at my side. The pick was used to gently rock the piton back and forth and then when it was in its center of the jam, it would pull out easily.

The first Owl was 60 feet and we rested at its top. Then we proceeded to the next owl that was 90 feet tall. The Swiss instructor kept telling us to look for tiny rock protrusions that he called "crystals." We did, but with our farmer boots, they sometimes were too small to assure solid footing. Both Mark and I each fell once. Secured with a safety line, the event was short but an eye-opener. It was only about 3 or 4 feet but it scared the over confidence right out of us. Each step and traverse was more carefully executed until we reached the top. We all took a rest on top on the great Owl and drank in the sights below. One hundred and fifty feet straight up was quite an accomplishment for a greenhorn I thought.

I then realized we must go down the same way we came up. It was steep on all sides of the Ear or Owl. We were now introduced to rappelling. This procedure entailed us to put on a seat harness. A carabineer was attached, with a brake bar, and rope.

The instructor then anchored all of this and the command to rappel was given. The daring climber backs towards the edge of the precipice and with a leap of faith, jumps backwards. Some of the rope that is about the waist is played out so that a short distance is descended before the body swings back to the rock's surface. With legs extended, the climber pushes off again and more rope is played out until the descent is completed. After the first backward leap, it soon becomes exhilarating and takes only seconds to complete. Several hours up and a few seconds down. A mountain climb in miniature, I thought, as the three of us regrouped at the base of the Owls. With, "wows," and other exclamations of joy my Son and I asked where a good first climb might be located. The expert climber said that the highest mountain in the National Park was located only a few miles from Estes Park. He said that Long's Peak would be a great first attempt to exhibit our new climbing skills without much danger. On our drive back to camp we agreed to get up early the next morning and climb Long's Peak.

Mark and I were up at the crack of dawn and loaded up our Yamaha 125 Enduro motorcycle that we had carried on the front of our Travelall during this vacation trip. With helmets on our heads and excitement in our breasts, we drove toward the base of the mountain on that cold morning in 1972. Shivering, we parked and locked the bike at the trailhead. We read all the posters and signs that the Park Service had placed for our edification. The daring duo then started up the trail with knapsack, canteen, and high expectations of fun and adventure.

The trailhead is at about 8000 feet, therefore the untrained and out of conditioned climber, soon notes that going up is a laborious task of increasing proportion. The first few miles and hours are spent on a well-defined trail, weaving itself through the beautiful pine forest and over meandering alpine streams. We note that the vegetation becomes smaller and sparser as we near an altitude of about 10,000 feet.

Soon we are above the tree line and begin to feel that we truly are on a mountain as the vistas open up and the air becomes thinner. Like plodding machines, we continue slowly, huffing and puffing in the rarefied atmosphere. We finally arrive at a place called the Boulder Field, where we had to stop, rest, and eat a little something. Looking up at the summit and recalling how many more feet we must climb, we begin to discuss our options. The morning had already burned away, now it was early afternoon, and I was bushed. Tired. Exhausted. I had a headache that wouldn't quit. I sat on a great boulder, just nibbling at some sustenance when I asked Mark if he would be disappointed if we canceled this trip and return to the base while I still had the strength and it was light? He said it would be OK with him and we therefore returned to the place from whence we came.

On the descent, I promised Mark, we would come back some day and climb this mountain to the top. I would prepare and train. I would quit smoking and drop some excess weight. We would take two days to do it and camp at the Boulder Field. We would buy new packs, shoes, and equipment to conquer this mighty mound or my name would be changed to Quitter.

Two years went bye in the wink of an eye. I had to fulfill my promise and therefore we set a time to go in the summer of 1974. I had started a new job only months before and the week off I needed was hard to come by. Finally, all of the arrangements were made and a time schedule formulated. New purchases were made almost daily until the August day came that signaled the beginning of the mountain climb. We packed all of our gear in the little VW, said our goodbyes, and headed towards Colorado. Driving from central Ohio to Estes Park was going to take us over 25 hours. Mark drove for a period of time and then I did the same. When we wanted some sleep, we curled up on the back seat of our little Fast Back Volkswagen and tried to sleep as the other adventurer drove.

We reached Estes Park, drove out to the trailhead, and spent the night at a little campsite at the base of the great mountain. The next morning, after very little sleep, we packed up and started our adventure for the second time. We knew that this time we could be more at ease and take our time. We would spend this night at a campsite near the great boulder field and then continue to the top the following day.

The trail started out as though it was just a little hiking path. It meandered through hardwoods and evergreens that covered the mountains' nakedness. Smooth and wide it progressed by way of little bridges across babbling brooks. A tranquil footpath that belied its upward ascent except by an occasional hairpin turn that demonstrated the cause of our now noticeable oxygen debt. Our original rapid fire, excitable conversation now was turning into shorter sentences that were produced with some exertion. We noticed our bodies leaning into the climb to keep our backpacks center of gravity adjusted to the more elevated pitch of our climb. Heads now lowered towards the ground with deep breathing to extract as much oxygen from the air as possible. Glances to the side now tell us that the vegetation had diminished. No longer any great trees to obscure the mountains truth. It was rocky and barren in spots therefore the higher elevations now easily came into better view. Twisting and turning the path became narrow and more demanding as we came out into a large area that was the tree line. No large woody vegetation beyond this elevation. Up ahead on the next plateau was Boulder Field and one of the campgrounds. To the left was Chasm Lake and a large snowfield. We could camp out in that vicinity. We stopped and rested several times and ate our lunch. Soon we came to a place that was below the snowfield. It had hundreds of clumps of grass that were surrounded by hundreds of tiny streams of water. The water was the result of the mini glacial or snowfield just above that continued to melt in the brief August sun. We finally located one of these clump-like islands that were large enough to accommodate us and pitched our tent. We set about unpacking and arranged our gear to stay the night.

After our housekeeping chores were completed we still had some of the afternoon and evening left to enjoy this part of the mountain. We headed down a narrow path that led to Chasm Lake. It was a small pocket of water that was crystal clear and icy cold in a niche of the high mountain.

We arrived and just sat around and drank in the clean air and beautiful vista. At the end of the tiny lake, the mountain raised straight up in a vertical wall that seemed to go to the very top of the mountain. We noticed a few alpine animals. The busy little Pika and a burrowing marmot were both entertaining and interesting. The pica pulls the green grasses and lays them in the sun on large rocks to dry. When dried the grass becomes hay that the rabbit like creature stores in deep burrows for winter hibernation and food. All was pure and pristine. I looked closely at the lake and was shocked to see that a beer can was lying on the bottom. Jolted back to reality we returned to the high alpine meadow that we would call home tonight. Seeing the snowfield from a distance, we decided to climb to the highest accessible part and slide down the sloping white mass. The field ended just above our little camp and we would be home free after an exhilarating ride.

Mark and I made our way to the top of the sloping snowfield. After climbing up on several boulders, we were able to transport ourselves to the inviting, slippery great white way that drew out our child-like spirits. The ride down continued with ever increasing speed as we approached the end of the snowfield. At the last second, we realized for the first time that the field was at least eight to ten feet above the soggy meadow that we had established our camp. Nothing left to do but to make a graceful leap into space and search out below us for a place to land that was not rocky or too wet. We both were fortunate to make good landings with nothing broken. At our new vantage point on the ground, we could see that the glacial was melting underneath and was for the most part a hollow shell. We could see great boulders as well as craters lurking beneath the snowfield. If we had fallen through on the slide down, it would have been disastrous.

The sun was going down and we quickly returned to camp. Mark was desirous to try out his freeze dried dinner He heated some water on our little propane stove and then added the packaged dried food and mixed. The water boils at a much lower temperature at this altitude, therefore it took longer before anything looked like food. I felt a little nauseated and did not partake. I tried some coffee and it didn't even seem to be very appetizing. Maybe I would feel better in the morning.

The night air on the mountain was quite crisp and made sounds that were unfamiliar to the flat Lander. I woke up every hour to check the time and see if Mark was sleeping well. All was in order.

First light came very early and we were both eager to get started. Mark scurried around and made breakfast and I tried my coffee and dried fruit. It didn't go well. We continued our chores to break camp and pack our backpacks to initiate the great climb.

We pulled out just after sun up and started the climb towards Boulder Field and the summit. Soon it became apparent that distances were quite deceiving. The altitude took all the energy I could exert just to keep my lungs gasping for air that had very little oxygen in it. I kept my head down and looked at the path beneath me. It slowly moved behind me at an agonizing pace. The pack on my back became heavier with each step. All thoughts became focused on how to make the climb easier and a flash of genius soon loomed before me.

"Mark," I called into the ever-increasing distance between us. "Lets stow our backpacks behind some rocks and get them on the way down. This will make our going much less difficult," I said to my agreeable son. We found some huge boulders and stashed our gear so that no one could easily detect them. Now this was much better I thought, as we again started off, sans unnecessary weighty paraphernalia. The going was easy through the boulder field. At this point, we could see the eye of the needle that was an opening on a high ridge that led to the backside of the mountain. We kept the needle in sight as we jumped and scramble over, through and around enormous boulders that lay strewn through out this high plateau. The surface of the moon couldn't have appeared more forbidding.

We finally reached the high part of the boulder field and entered the keyhole, thereby passing from the front of the mountain to the back. The guide book said to be on the look out for the painted targets on rock formations to lead us up the back side to a higher point that would then lets us return to the front face of Long's Peak. The painted circular targets were painted in yellow and white. They were aptly nicknamed the fried eggs of Long's Peak.

At first, they were easy to locate but as the morning progressed and as we ascended to higher elevations, the identifications became more difficult. I think the painter got as tired as we were, making smaller eggs, and using less paint. This hardship aggravated our progress, because several times we went in divergent directions only to see a target painted on rock that was almost unnoticeable from our previous location. We were guessing. To prevent some duplication of exertion, Mark would go far ahead to determine that the way was correct.

Slowly the morning wore on and I was experiencing altitude sickness. I had brought some granola but was unable to keep it down. My head was splitting with pain. My legs and lungs were crying out for relief as they burned and ached alternately. I finally came to the agonizing decision that I wasn't going to make it to the top. I couldn't even see the top, as great cliffs and boulders hid it yet to be navigated. I reluctantly began to wave to Mark to return. He was so far up that my voice was carried away by the wind when I tried to communicate by yelling. With arms waving and a painful grimace upon my face I tried again and again to inform my son to return to his ailing father. Each time the response from Mark was more arm waving and then turning to climb even higher. He certainly couldn't see my face from that distance. I reacted by accelerating my climb to catch up with him to relate my condition and decree to return.

I continued to climb with all the strength of the giants of pride and image that were in me. It was bad enough that I failed two years ago and to quit now was very hard to do in front of my eldest son. After all, we had planned, trained, and attacked from our own vantage points this time. Our conquest was to be denied I thought as the pain and suffering increased. Mark continued higher and higher and glanced back at his dying father less and less. He disappeared.

Up and up the backside of the mountain until a high ridge was gained. The fried eggs now behind me I found myself upon a narrow, grooved path, cut into the rock and stone on the front side of the mountain. On the left, the rock went straight up and on the right it went straight down. I carefully moved along the rut looking for my lost companion. The path moved around the mountain and no one was in sight. I noticed some water trickling down the face of the great rock and because of my dehydrated condition began to draw water into me. This face to lips contact with Long's Peak seemed to revive me for a few minutes. My stomach noticed the intrusion and reacted violently. My second state being worst that the former I eventually had to lie prostrate in the depression of the mountain trail.

Here I remained in pain and discomfort. My thoughts were on Mark and his progress. Surely, he would return after his final ascent to help his old father back down this hill of despair. Maybe I would die and they would have to send a helicopter to bring my body down, thereby saving me the agony. Soon, I won't even have to walk down, as my head must now be the approximate size of the mountain. I continued to wallow in the pits of self-pity and anguish. Surely, no one can help. Suddenly I heard voices.

Two feminine voices, dripping with concern and pathos came wafting upon alpine wings to my surprised ears. I was not alone on the path. Someone knelt beside me and asked me if I was all right. Of course I was, I replied as I returned to the world of reality. I turned and looked to see two women bending close to determine the extent of my condition. "Would you like some candy?" One of my benefactors asked. "No, I can't keep anything down," I responded. "How about some raisins or chewing gum?" The other agent of mercy inquired

. "I'll try some gum," I uttered in hope.

Soon we exchanged information about who we were and what we were doing. I concluded with the request that they go on and inform Mark of my situation and for him to return when he had finished his climb. With reassurances all around and heartfelt thanks, they left. Two retired teachers on a quest. Quickly and quietly, they soon disappeared around the curvature of the mountain and I was alone again.

I continued to pray as I had all the way up the mountain that my resolve to conquer this mountain would not be so vigorously challenged. I chewed the gum and little by little, my strength came back. The sugar and chewing activity, along with my renewed prayers raised me up to my feet. The rest had helped, as my second wind came back to propel me forward towards the apex of this mountain. Something deep inside me also helped.

In less than an hour of following, the trail it ended. Only a large arrow painted on the side of the rock pointing up welcomed me at this high juncture. Looking up I could make out the forms of two people completing the climb and scrambling onto the tabletop peak. They were most likely my two earlier acquaintances. The climb was up a sheer rock face about 90 to 100 feet high. I started up with the thought if those two ladies could make it, so could I. Occasionally I would look back down and be reminded that one false move would send me straight down and to a quick death. Keeping my body close to the rock, I would inch by inch ascend the steep incline. A little ledge here and a rock crystal there to afford a toe or finger hold. Up and up I went struggling but determined. Soon I was to hear the voice of several successful climbers coming down. One voice was saying how much fun it was and the other voice was agreeing. Looking up I see that the first voice came from a ten-year-old boy. I was encouraged and humiliated. I pushed upward with more fervor than before and soon was being helped by Mark for the final lift on to the peaks zenith. It was a nearly square area of perhaps 25feet. The surface was relatively flat. Mark led me over to the center where a pipe had been embedded that contained a scroll for the registration of the successful climbers names. I lifted the cap of the pipe and entered my name on the registry just below Mark's name. It was done. On top of the world, it seemed at 14,264 feet above sea level. The vista in all directions was breath taking and beautiful. I saw a fly. How did he get here, I thought.

After a few minutes, I felt a sudden and compulsive urge to get down. I went to the center of the peak and lay down. I told Mark to look around a while and then we would have to be going. It was already afternoon and the day was going fast. Soon Mark was ready and I left my spread eagle position and forced myself to look down that steep incline. We had to turn around and descend backwards. Feeling and groping for small spaces that would support our weight we left Long's Peak. Leaving behind that mixed feeling of accomplishment and expectation we returned to the narrow channeled pathway that lead to the target zone. We now moved as experienced climbers through the fried egg zone. The gathering of clouds began to move upon the mountain. Gusts of wind, that were unnaturally chilly for the summer, burst upon us from time to time. The moves came quicker now and with less exertion than when we were climbing. Spatters of rain began to throw themselves upon us as we sighted the keyhole. Distances in the mountains can be deceiving. The velocity of the wind picked up and was full of sleet as it stung our faces. We finally reached the keyhole and noticed and remembered at the same time, the stone cabin to our right. It was built for just such an occasion. We headed for it as the weather continued to increase, now with the presence of snow. We reached the little stone hut and entered to find a small assembly of hikers and climbers. It was soon apparent to me, as I smelled the huddled body odors in that damp enclosure that I must continue. I told Mark that I was going on and would wait for him at the place we had stashed our backpacks. With out another word I reentered the elements and continued to navigate the boulder field. Jumping from one huge boulder to the next I preceded to move down the boulder field. Each rock was gigantic and had many crevices that I could fall into and no one would be able to find me. All around me a meteorological frenzy was happening. Lightening and thunder were continuous as the snow whipped around me only to find rain and sleet on the other side. The wind seemed to lift me from one boulder to the next like so much straw. In the middle of the boulder field a great clap of thunder that sounded like a thousand explosions shook me enough to look around to see what was happening. I saw lightning all around me with little blue leftovers that danced on the huge stones. Finally, one of them touched me and gave a great tingling sensation that reminded me that I was where I shouldn't be. A few more leaps and I saw a place where I could jump down and take cover. Down and in between the boulders I went to wait out the mountains revenge. I had prayed more than once on this trip. I did so again. Soon the weather abated and it wasn't too long until I heard the voices of those released from the confines of the high stone cabin. Mark was in the front and coming right towards me. We were soon reunited and on our way to retrieve our backpacks. I still was very weak and told Mark that we would get a motel for the night to rest up. He agreed. We reached the bottom of the mountain in about four hours total. Much easier coming down than going up. We left the trailhead, found a motel, and settled in. I had a cola and slept for about an hour. When I awoke, I felt Like a new person. I suggested to Mark that we go out to a nice restaurant and get a good meal. He was very agreeable since we had not eaten for such a long period. We went out and ordered Mountain rainbow trout. The waitress showed Mark how to get the meat off the bones and not waste any meat. We talked and had a good time. We returned to the motel and were both ready to hit the sack. I asked Mark if he had a good time and he answered in the affirmative. Little did I know how much this climb touched him until later that night? I awoke to hear Mark talking in his sleep. I moved closer and listened carefully. "I think I'll climb the highest points in all the states," he muttered in his sleep. I guess he did enjoy the climb.

The End

RUSTY GUN

IT WAS A SATURDAY. BUSINESS was slow at my drug store. Since it was early December, the air was both cold and moist. It also was pitch black outside even though it was only 6 P.M. I looked out through the front door to try to find that elusive and invisible customer who was never there. Nevertheless, I looked anyhow. What I saw was little piles of half melted snow still scattered around the parking lot in that half dirty, half glistening icy residue of an empty winter parking lot.

I went to the cash register and in a methodically set of reestablished movements, counted out the days receipts and reset the register. I quickly looked about to make sure no one was looking and put the cash and other pertinent material in a bag to carry back to my little area of the Pharmacy were I was able to do the book keeping and banking. My clerk Brenda was busy putting cards away and occasionally waiting on the store's few customers. Some of the customers would shout a word of recognition back to me and wave. Some would stomp off the excess snow and that turned to puddled water with a comment that the cold wet evening was no fun to be out in. Some would talk in low voices trying to get Brenda to giggle or act surprised in that most precious of ways that young girls have.

I could tell it was going to be another long evening. My wife and family were at some Holiday gathering again having a good time without me. A Drug Store owner's lot was getting lonelier each year. The big Drug chains were getting bigger and expanding to the point it seemed like nothing was happening at the so called Corner Drug Store anymore. I began to feel sorry for myself again and knew that looking at the sparse receipts of the day would only add to my dilemma. Another few months like these were threatening to take me over the edge of despair. When my thoughts were darkest and my mood deepest I was aware of Brenda standing next to me." Snap out of it boy," I said to myself. "You have a responsibility and a store to run."

Dick, what should I do with these soiled greeting cards"? Brenda's voice snapped me out of my blue funk. With all my problems, nothing else could possibly go wrong and besides I beheld a young girl in my employ that was concerned with soiled greeting cards. It was a pleasure to teach young people the routine of small community retailing. I thought as I began to show Brenda the procedure to return greeting cards to the Card Company that maybe all this is worthwhile after all. I looked up to see a tall customer standing in the center of my small store. He was about 25 feet away from us and looking towards the front of the store. He seemed bewildered or confused, even though I could only see the brightly colored bands of his ski headgear. I thought if he turned towards us, I would ask if we could help him. Since after a few seconds he did not turn around, I told Brenda to go out on the floor and ask if we could assist him in finding any of our drug store items. She left the slightly elevated Pharmacy area and walked towards our tall gentleman customer. I saw Brenda freeze as she reached a place that was in front of him and began to mumble in muffled tones. It was then that he glanced back at me and I saw for the first time the eerie and frightening full face of the ski mask. He looked back at Brenda quickly and made a motion to her that revealed to me, as my heart began to race, that a sawed off rusty shotgun was his menacing companion. Brenda was frozen with fear and could not move or speak at that instant. A thousand thoughts and pictures ran through my mind as I reached down under the Pharmacy counter and pushed what we called the panic button. This was installed for just such an occasion. It quietly alerted a security company that a hold-up was taking place and to contact the Police on our behalf. The panic button now pushed, my hand slipped into a drawer were I kept a loaded 38 Police Special S & W. Revolver. I kept an eye peeled on our visitor and moved not a muscle that could be seen or detected as threatening. Rusty Shotgun kept trying to get Brenda to respond to some sort of command that appeared too difficult for her to comprehend. He looked back at me once or twice but was intent on Brenda biding his commands. My hand went up like lightning with its small but deadly 38 revolver aimed directly at Rusty Shotgun's keeper.

I had purchased this gun ten years before in a little town where I had owned my first Drug Store. At that drugstore I was burglarized several times but had never been held up. Ten years ago I was younger and less likely to think about the possibility of a real human target. The first store had hard tile floors. Easy to clean up. This store had nice green carpeting. It would be a mess to clean up after. How about the bad publicity that goes with a store that has had a killing in it. Suppose this man has a relative that will get EVEN and do me in. Or possibly a member of my family would be put in jeopardy. How about all the paper work that I would have to be filled out tonight. I would have to tell my wife and Pastor the dastardly thing I had committed. My finger still on the trigger and the sights still full of one head in a ski mask I came to the decision that I couldn't do it today. With one fluid motion my hand came down, I placed the revolver in the drawer, and blurted out, "May I help you"? I moved off the Pharmacy platform and down the aisle with my hands half held out with palms toward old Rusty Gun. I looked up in those cut out places where two eyes were hiding and saw more fear than intelligence. I told Brenda to come with us and to get a bag. I asked Rusty if he wanted all the money that was in the cash register. He nodded and mumbled in the affirmative and we all moved in unison towards the front cash register like a comic opera. Weenie,

Meanie and Doe. Brenda reached under the counter and I thought Rusty would have a coronary. He bit into the mouth border of the facemask and uttered oaths thinking Brenda was not just getting a paper bag. She brought out the bag and showed him it was not loaded and proceeded to fill it with the money left in the register. I asked if the change would also be acceptable and it was. When all the money was in the bag Ski Mask got serious and waved the gun towards a space on the floor behind some shelving and motioned for us to lie down on our stomachs. I again let my thoughts fly through the pages of Real Detective and other such books that have the robber shoot the victims in the back as they lay on the cold floor. Even though ours was carpeted I spoke up and Said "If you are going to shoot me, do it while I am Standing up." (Oh Fool) His dull eyes glazed over with anger and he anxiously motioned with the rusty shotgun for me to lie down as Brenda had done as he barked, "do not get up for 5 minutes." As he put old Rusty's barrel at the nape of my neck I was quiet and obedient. I soon heard the big front door close with a soft swoosh of the pneumatic door closer. All was quiet for a moment. No cars, or car doors slamming. No popping off with a bang as Rusty might have done in a victory gesture. No voices or hurried commands. Nothing except the slow beginning of sobbing coming from the body next to me. Brenda had had it. The sobbing began to increase with total body involvement to the point that I felt I must get up and slap her back to reality. It was then I heard the sound of doors opening and voices and as I turned over, the familiar click, click sound as the red light on the roof of the Police cruiser pulsated into the room. In came the Police with guns drawn and questions galore. It was over. "He just left out that door," I said, in answer to one question. "Yes we are all right." in, answer to the next. After some more questions and forms to fill out, I closed the Store. The police took, totally limp, Brenda home.

As I was leaving I was thinking that only a short time earlier I was complaining and in near despair. This life isn't so bad. The robber was just scared and out of money. Maybe the gun wasn't even loaded. As I was in my car ready to leave when a policeman came up to the car and showed me the live shotgun cartridge they had found in the alley. The gun was *loaded*. I was fortunate. Things worse than slow nights and a dying store are out there. A dead husband and father would not be going home to a wife and family that really cared and no killer was going home for the Holidays. Dick and ski mask were both blessed that night.

The End